A Beth-Hill Novella: Karen Montgomery Series, Book 4: Detour

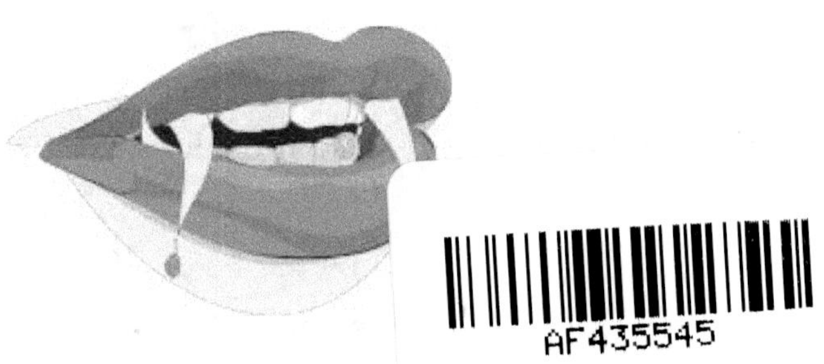

By Jennifer St. Clair

Writers Exchange E-Publishing

http://www.writers-exchange.com

A Beth-Hill Novel: Karen Montgomery Series Book 4: Detour
Copyright 2012, 2015, 2023 Jennifer St. Clair
Writers Exchange E-Publishing
PO Box 372
ATHERTON QLD 4883

Cover Art by: Jatin

Published by Writers Exchange E-Publishing
http://www.writers-exchange.com

Dedication

Dedicated to Elsa, just because.

Chapter 1

I'm on automatic pilot in the mornings.

If anyone is planning my death, or to 'take me down' (or whatever the current vernacular is today), I'd suggest they make their attempt in the morning as I'm stumbling through my tasks before I leave for work, or maybe while I'm driving for work, since I'm usually on automatic pilot by then, listening to NPR or putting my thoughts in order for the day.

That's going to be my excuse for why I didn't remember about the detour; it was difficult enough for me to remember a meeting at another location first thing on Monday morning (and I was the one who had suggested it, so it was only my fault.) And since spring had barely begun to arrive, it was still dark in the mornings, and my car automatically swung towards my usual route, down the main road and not towards the go-around like it should have been.

I really didn't realize anything was wrong until I saw the first flashing sign, and then my caffeine-addled brain caught up with current events and I remembered vaguely hearing something about a bridge out and a detour that took twenty minutes to get around. Which would, of course make me late for the meeting.

I pulled over right in front of the detour sign, but my cell phone didn't have any service and I had--in a fit of what now seemed like stupidity--refused to let Russ place a spell on my cell phone so that wouldn't happen. I can't remember what my argument had been, but it had sounded plausible at the time.

There was a little side road right before the detour, but I had no idea where it led, and even less of an idea where I'd end up if I took it instead of the 'official' detour. But still, if I could find a quick way around, it would save me some time and embarrassment, so I turned my car down the side road and left the flashing signs behind.

Right then, of course, it started to rain.

We'd just had a month of snow and rain and ice and rain again, so the ditches on either side of this road were swollen and full, and in some places, had erupted from their banks to spread across the road and mingle in the middle. I know just as well as anyone that you're not supposed to drive through rushing water, but what else could I have done?

And as I inched along the road, hoping for another side road with less flooding, I realized that I hadn't seen a single light from any house on either side of the road since I'd first turned down this 'shortcut'. Trees pressed close against the pavement where the ditches had filled with silt and mud over the years, and the shine of my headlights were the only lights to pierce the cloying darkness.

And had it gotten darker? I glanced at the clock on the dashboard, it was eight in the morning, and it looked like midnight outside.

I kept going, inching slowly down a hill, through six inches of rushing water, realizing, somewhere in the back of my mind that I shouldn't have come here; I should have turned around and gotten to the meeting late, rather than never arrive at all.

But it was too to turn back now. I drove down the middle of the road with my brights on and my windshield wipers running on full blast, until I reached what was, for me, the end of the road.

At one point, the bridge had been accessible, but as it is with many small rural routes, upkeep had not been on the township trustees priority list. The bridge had washed out a long time ago; the road ended in a jagged chunk of asphalt that was, even now, flaking away into the raging water. The rusting hulk of a car stuck up out of the middle, as if someone, long ago, had tried to pass and had never reached their destination.

On the other side, the road meandered upward and vanished into the trees. On my side, the only sign of habitation was a white wooden cross--like the ones that appear at the scene of fatal accidents--fairly glowing in the darkness.

My cell phone beeped. Without taking my eyes off the raging river, I picked it up, dialed Russ' number by heart, and listened to it ring. That's when I saw the man standing beside the cross, one hand resting on the top of it as if he had all the time in the world. Staring, of course. Right at me.

I disconnected the call as he stepped onto the road and made his way across. He wasn't exactly dressed for the weather; he wore a light corduroy jacket, now soaking wet, and a leather hat. Jeans, boots that weren't quite hiking boots; he touched my car's hood as if to assure himself it was really there, then moved to my window.

At least the rain had lessened a bit, I thought, as I rolled it down enough to talk.

"The road's out," he said before I could speak. Even up close I couldn't get a good look at his face; his hat cast it in shadow.

"I see that," I said. "Do you know if there's a driveway or anything where I could turn around?"

The man pointed towards the cross, and I saw a gravel drive leading deeper into the forest; presumably towards his house. "If you turn around there, you should be able to get back to the main road."

"Thank you," I said, and when he didn't move, I said, "I appreciate your kindness."

The man blinked at me. "Kindness?"

"You didn't have to come all the way out here in the rain to tell me the road was out," I said. As the rain lessened, the sky grew lighter, more akin to morning now and not night. Thunder rumbled in the distance, a low grumbling as if the storm itself protested moving away.

"It wasn't that far," he said, and glanced up at the sky.

And for the first time, I saw the man's face clearly.

I didn't recognize him, but he seemed familiar nonetheless. Greying ginger hair peeked out from under his hat; his eyes were pale, either hazel or green, I couldn't tell. But he seemed the type to burn in the sunlight; more suited behind a desk than outdoors.

I stuck out my own hand. "Karen Montgomery."

He stared at it for a moment, then touched my hand with his. "Sam. Sam Rose." His hands were workman's hands, seamed and calloused.

"I appreciate your kindness, Mr. Rose," I said, and this time, he stepped away from my car and retreated back to the cross to watch me attempt to back up and turn around, now that--was that the *sun?*--the storm seemed to be over.

When I glanced back at the cross, Sam Rose was gone and the painted wood that had seemed so flawless in the darkness was now weathered and worn and listing to one side. Even the raging water seemed calmer; but the car had not changed. It was still a rusting wreck, forever drowning in the creekbed, forgotten like the road.

With weak sunlight sparkling off my windshield and the water draining quickly from the road ahead, I made my way back to the detour, and then back to the main highway. I was only thirty minutes late for my meeting, and by lunchtime, the terror of the morning had faded enough so I could joke about it to Russ when we met for lunch.

Chapter 2

"**B**ut there *aren't* any side roads off the main road," he said when I finished my story. "That's why the detour is so annoying. Did you know it extends into Faerie? That's right on the edge of the Veil."

"It did kind of seem like the road time forgot," I said, remembering the lack of civilization. "And now that you mention it, I don't remember seeing any telephone poles, either."

"And yet there's someone living out there," Russ said, and took a careful bite of his soup. Despite the fact that he'd moved out of my apartment and, under protest, into an actual *house* as opposed to his van, he still wasn't completely healed. "Which makes me wonder if the person you saw was human."

"Does it matter if he was?" I asked. "He was real enough; he shook--well, touched, I guess--my hand."

"Even so," he said, and took another bite when the first one didn't seem to disagree with him. "And it wasn't raining this morning, either. At least not here."

"That's what they call a pop-up thunderstorm," I said. "And wouldn't I *notice* if I slipped through the Veil?"

"You might," Russ said. "And you might not. It depends. And you did say it was raining quite a bit by then; and maybe the road you were on only appears in this world when it rains. Who knows?"

"I wonder where it comes out on the other side?" I asked, innocently enough, but he stopped with his spoon halfway to his lips and stared at me.

"Promise me you won't go exploring," Russ said. "Please."

"I won't go exploring without you, at least," I told him. "And I promise."

He seemed to be happy enough with that, so we changed the subject to houses, because that was my other project of date; finding a permanent place to live.

Russ' house had been loaned to him by the Council; loaned indefinitely, with the express expectation that he would join them when he was healed enough to report for duty. He hadn't made any sort of decision yet as far as I knew, but there'd been other movement; the talk of teaching at Darkbrook wasn't just talk anymore, and the discussion about the new classes had brought back a bit of his previous vigor.

Since he'd spent the first two weeks of his convalescence holed up in my apartment, barely speaking to anyone, this was a marked improvement.

House hunting for me, however, had been a bit trickier. I had never quite realized it before, but I was a very picky person, and my realtor was about to throw in the towel and declare it a day.

The offer stood on the table to move in with Russ--his offer, my refusal-- but I wanted to give him a chance to recover and settle in before I pushed myself into his life any further.

At least, that's what I told myself. And sometimes I believed it.

"No luck?" Russ' voice brought me out of my reverie. "I know you said you were going to look at houses over the weekend..."

"One was too remodeled, and one was not remodeled enough," I said. "I draw the line at having to pump my own water, and I'm rather fond of electricity."

"Lucas said the house next door to mine, to the one I'm staying in, is for sale," Russ said, and fastened his gaze on his soup and not me.

"It might as well be yours," I said. "I don't think they're intending to let you leave."

Russ smiled. "It's nice to be wanted," he said, and I realized--after a moment of shock--that he was serious. "For a change."

"This house," I prompted. "What does it look like?"

"The house I'm staying in used to be the carriage house," Russ said. "So it's big, but not a mansion. I'm sure it would be horrible to heat in the winter, but maybe we could get around that, close off a few rooms or something."

"Rig up a spell or two," I suggested, and he hesitated, then shrugged.

"Perhaps. I'd have to see. I'm not very good at heat, but I'm sure I could learn."

"You've seen this house?" I asked. And then, because he hadn't said, "Who owns it?"

"There's a library," Russ said, and I knew he was baiting me now, because *he* knew I couldn't resist a library. *Any* library. "And it's practically furnished."

"And?" I asked. "What's the catch? It's falling down? Or haunted?" I thought I could handle haunted; after all, the library was haunted.

"No." Russ spoke slowly, as if trying to choose the right words. "Neither falling down nor haunted. Not in the traditional sense, at least."

"Then what?" I glanced at my watch. "I have to drop you off anyway-- and I have time to drive past it, at least--I didn't even know there *was* a house next door to yours."

"It's not mine," Russ said. "It belongs to the Council, and so does the house next door." He still wouldn't look at me; his face was drawn and pale now, as if he'd overextended himself. "I've been walking a bit in the woods during the day."

"It's kind of cold to be doing that, isn't it?" I asked, then immediately regretted my words, because that had been the reason why he'd moved out of my apartment so soon. Both Lucas and Sennet had been against it, and Lucas had even gone so far as to take away the keys to his van. Temporarily.

"What *else* am I supposed to do?" he asked, but he wasn't angry; more dejected. "I can't--" He covered his face with his hands.

"The last two times we've met, you haven't had your computer," I said. "And I noticed your van was gone."

"Lucas has my computer. My *computers*. All of them. And the van." Russ' voice was muffled. "The poison was a magically induced poison. Sennet thinks the reason why I'm not completely healed is because the poison feeds on magic. My talent. And if I don't use any magic; then I'll be okay."

"For how long?" I asked, horrified that he hadn't told me this before. He was so *reliant* on his talent. Much more than Lucas, or any of the other wizards I had met.

"Until the end of the month," Russ said, and lowered his hands. "Three more weeks. And then we'll see."

His gaze was bleak; it was almost as if Lucas and Sennet had saddled him with a life sentence instead of a mere respite. But then again, if I compared Russ' talent to my love of books, and if I tried to imagine not *reading* for three weeks...

"You should have told me sooner," I said, gently.

"I didn't want you to think that I was helpless," Russ said, and pushed the half-full bowl of soup away. "Or that I was broken beyond repair. Do you know how difficult it is for me to rely on other people for *everything?*"

"I was beginning to figure that part out," I said, but I kept my voice light, because I knew how he would react. And he did just as I expected; he flushed, then glanced at me, and then, finally, smiled.

"I'm sorry," he said. "I should have told you. After everything you've done for me, I owe--"

"No." I reached out and covered his clenched hand with my own. "We've been over this."

"It's very hard for me to ask for help," Russ said. "I've been by myself for a long time."

"I know," I said. "Do you want me to call in for the rest of the day? There's nothing pressing at the library that I have to deal with this afternoon."

"No book thieves?" Russ asked, trying, and failing, to make light of his distress.

"Say the word," I told him, completely serious. "And I'll spend the rest of the day with you."

At first, I thought he would refuse; that he'd continue to pretend everything was fine. But then he took a deep breath and nodded. "Yes. I would love it if you spent the rest of the day with me."

I pulled out my cell phone, dialed the library's number, left a message for Penny, and closed it back up. "Done."

"We could drive by the house," Russ suggested.

At that very moment, I could have cared less about the house. "Will you answer one question for me?"

His gaze grew hooded; his mouth thinned. "Just one?"

"Just one. Is this fatal?"

He hadn't expected *that* question. "What?"

I picked up the check and folded my arms. "You heard me."

"Sennet doesn't think so," he said.

"What do *you* think?" I asked.

He considered that question very carefully. "I know that when I kept waking up in pain I thought it might be," he said. "But for the past week, it's been much better."

"Without magic," I said.

"Yes."

"That would be the hardest thing I've ever done in my life," I said, and his gaze cleared. Did no one else realize how much he relied on his talents? Gabriel might, I thought; the Master of the Hunt seemed to know quite a bit about Russell Moore. But Gabriel held his own counsel; he wasn't one to gossip.

"Yes." He spoke quickly, almost running the words together in his haste to get them out. "Lucas doesn't understand. Sennet just expects me to be able to *ignore* everything; it's like trying to stop breathing!"

I glanced outside. It was cloudy, overcast, a damp early spring day in Ohio. "What else can you do to keep your mind off your talents?"

"That's why I've been walking," Russ admitted. "Without any sort of technology nearby, it's easier to not use it."

"Then are you up for a walk?" I asked.

"Of course," Russ said. "Where to?"

"It's starting to rain," I told him.

"You want to go walking in the rain?" He glanced outside, confused, but then his face cleared. "You want to go look at your detour."

"If you don't think it would be safe, we won't go," I said.

"Safe." Absently, he stole one of my french fries and popped it in his mouth. "Without a torrential downpour, it should be safe enough. I don't have to do any magic to get in and out of Faerie."

"We don't *have* to go," I said.

Russ smiled. This time, his smile reached his eyes. "Yes, we do, if only to satisfy your curiosity, and mine."

"I'm glad you're curious," I said.

"It beats the alternative," Russ replied, and snatched the check out of my hand.

"Hey!"

He shook his head. "You always pay. I'm *not* penniless."

"I never said you were," I said, amused. "But *I* have a job."

"And *I'll* have one once we get things set up at Darkbrook," Russ replied. "And I'm saving all sorts of money on gas not driving the van."

"Knowing your van, I bet you are," I said, and surrendered. "At least let me leave a tip."

Twenty minutes later, we were on our way down the road and Russ sat beside me, his fingers drumming on his knees, more relaxed than he had been in weeks.

And I realized the reason for his reticence, it wasn't only that he'd been afraid I would abandon him. It was because I'd let him go.

"Your house isn't big enough for my library," I said, breaking the monotonous sound of the windshield wipers. "And you need your space, just as I need mine. If I bought the house next door--"

Russ' fingers stilled. "I haven't told you everything about the house next door," he said.

"Then tell me," I suggested, but we were at the detour now, and the little road--hardly more than a pathway--stretched into the trees.

"Huh," Russ said, and straightened up in his seat. "It's not that I didn't believe you, but...this isn't supposed to be here. I've looked at the maps. There are no streets this close to the bridge. I'd swear it."

"Maps aren't always right," I told him, and turned down the narrow lane. The rain briefly strengthened, then subsided into a drizzle again. "I didn't meet anyone coming the other way this morning."

"I'd imagine not," Russ said, and craned his head sideways to look at the tops of the trees. "No electric lines. No telephone poles. 'The road that time forgot'." And then, as the creek came into view, "Oh. I see what you mean."

The rusting car was still there, sticking up out of rushing water, although the rapids were gone by now. On the other side of the creek, the road still went straight up into the forest without a single glimpse of its destination.

"You know, I think it would be worse to come across this from the other side," Russ said. "Especially if the road was slippery, or it was dark outside."

I tried to imagine cresting a hill and seeing nothing below me. "Maybe that's what happened to the driver of the car."

"Then why would the cross be on *this* side?" Russ asked, and we sat in silence for a moment, staring down at the car. "Where's the driveway?"

"Right past--" I pointed towards the cross, but the driveway wasn't there. "It was a gravel driveway. Right there. I swear."

"There's no need to swear," Russ said, distractedly. "I believe you."

I glanced at him; his face was pale again, his lips pressed into a thin line. "Are you okay?"

"Yes." He fairly whispered the word. "And no." He opened the car door and lurched out with his hand over his mouth; I followed him into the spitting rain.

He knelt on the road on the other side of the car, doubled over, his arms now wrapped around his stomach. When he saw me, he waved me away; his movements jerky, his lips twisting in a grimace.

"I'll be fine." He gasped the words, though, and slipped when he tried to rise.

"Let me help you," I said, and held out my hand. "Please."

He let me take his arm, and let me help him up. He trembled against me, his hair damp against my cheek as I held him upright.

Behind him, I saw the gravel drive appear, almost like a rainbow appears after a storm, spreading through the dense trees until it seemed as if it had *always* been there; and we had just missed seeing it and nothing more.

"Tell me," I said, softly. That was the first time I'd really held him since he'd moved, and he seemed all skin and bones, all angles, wasting away in my arms.

He took a shallow breath, and then a deeper one when nothing happened. "I'm not dying."

"You sound like you're trying to convince yourself of that," I said, and he straightened up, staggering a little when he tried to stand on his own.

"Maybe I am." He leaned against the car, facing the cross and the driveway, although it took him a moment to see it. "Hey!"

"It appeared while you were indisposed," I said, and folded my arms. "Tell me."

"For the past few years, I've been living on potions that humans aren't supposed to be able to stomach," Russ said, a little color returning to his cheeks. "The 'restorative'."

"Josiah said it smelled like blood," I said, remembering.

"That's only part of it," Russ said. "It's more sorcery than magic. And there's a price to be paid for sorcery."

"What kind of a price?" I asked.

"I can't eat," Russ said. "It *hurts* to eat. But I can't just stop eating; I have to have some sort of sustenance."

"But not your restorative," I guessed. "You don't want to make more of it? Or you can't?"

"I can't." Russ sighed and wiped one hand across his face. "And it's not that I don't want to. I *can't*. Going back...going back would be worse."

"So you go cold turkey and suffer the consequences," I said. "Like the people who try to quit smoking?"

"Like the people who try to quit heroin," Russ said.

"Do they have AA meetings for recovering sorcerers?" I asked.

That startled a laugh out of him. "No. But maybe they should."

"So what *can* you eat?" I asked. "Have you been going to lunch with me and eating normal food just to be polite?"

The guilt in his gaze answered my question long before he replied. "Yes." He hesitated. "That's the only time I can spend time with you."

I opened my mouth to reply, perhaps inanely, and he stepped forward, touched one side of my cheek, and kissed me.

"This is neither a lover's lane nor a trysting spot," a voice said from behind us, slightly annoyed.

Russ stiffened and pulled away. I spun around to face Sam Rose, of course; I'd recognized his voice. He still wore the same clothes as this morning, his hat pulled down to shade his eyes.

"This is not a public road?" Russ asked, struggling for dignity.

Sam Rose opened his mouth to reply, but the sun broke through the clouds at the very same moment, washing the driveway, the cross, and the road, in weak light.

And he vanished, just as quickly as he had appeared.

Russ sagged back against my car. I took his arm; he nodded, his gaze on the driveway, not me.

"A ghost."

"A ghost?" I stared at the cross. "A ghost that appears only when it rains?"

"If he died in the rain, then he might appear in the rain," Russ said. "It's not uncommon for ghosts to be tied to the crosses; I'm sure their relatives don't realize how powerful a symbol a cross truly is."

"But what about the road?" I asked. "And the driveway? It's still there." I'd seen the crosses before, of course; everyone has. They pop up at the scenes of accidents, almost as if by magic. By magic...

"I don't know," Russ admitted. "That's part of what I don't understand."

"And how could he have touched me?" I asked.

"Was it raining when he touched you?" Russ asked.

"Yes."

"Hmm." He walked across the road, steady on his feet now, and stood at the edge of the driveway, his hands tucked in his jacket pockets, his eyes closed. "I don't feel any magic here. And we're not in Faerie, either."

"So it just appears and disappears by itself?" I asked, skeptical.

"I...I don't know," Russ said. "I don't know if it's a byproduct of your ghost, or if there's something else going on; if I were stronger, I'd use my computer to see if there's something I'm missing."

A light splatter of rain blew down from the trees. Clouds hid the sun again; Russ stepped away from the cross, towards me, and I saw him hesitate as he stepped onto the asphalt. And then, almost in slow motion, he fell forward, as if something had pushed him from behind. He landed hard, but rolled, and I started towards him as the rain fell harder, a downpour now, closer to how it had been before.

Sam Rose reached him before I did, and Russ stared up at his outstretched hand with no small amount of suspicion.

"Perhaps you should allow me to help you up before the sun shines again," he suggested.

Without speaking, Russ extended his hand, his eyes widening when Sam Rose's hand closed over his. And he seemed to have no trouble pulling him up; in fact, he seemed more solid in the rain. More...imposing. More aware.

"Did you push me?" Russ asked, his tone civil; he stepped back and almost fell again. This time, I caught his arm before he could fall.

"No." I thought I saw a glint of amusement in Sam Rose's gaze. "She pushed you *out*. Your lady--" He glanced at me. "Miss Montgomery was in her car earlier. That ensures some protection."

"'She'?" Russ asked.

"You have a...*taint*," Sam Rose said, ignoring Russ' question. He wiped his hand on his jacket, almost unconsciously, and took a step backwards.

"Yes, I know," Russ said. "I'm doing my best to get rid of it. Who is 'she'?"

"One of those who abide here," Sam Rose said, and indicated the driveway. "One of those who protect this place."

"Ghosts?" I asked.

Sam Rose shrugged. "Not as such."

I pointed to the car sticking up out of the middle of the creek. "Was that your car?"

He glanced towards the creek, and a strange, almost longing expression passed across his face. "Once, yes."

"How long have you been here?" Russ asked, and then, before Sam could answer, "Are *you* a ghost?"

I half-expected the sun to emerge from the clouds, but it did not; the rain continued, although not quite as hard. Still, with Russ' weakness and everything else he'd told me, I knew that it wasn't a good idea for him to stay out in the weather for a prolonged period of time. But he showed no sign of wanting to leave.

"I am not certain a taint such as yours can be 'gotten rid of'," Sam Rose said. "That is usually something present for life."

Russ waited a beat, then deliberately stepped forward, onto the driveway, his gaze locked on Sam Rose, as if waiting for him to protest, or do something to stop him.

"Are you usually so rude?" a voice asked, coming from nowhere and everywhere around us, a girl's voice, peeved.

"No," Russ replied. "Not usually. Just curious."

I glanced at Sam Rose; he was standing by the cross, looking alternately annoyed and curious himself.

"Would you show yourself to us?" I asked.

Sam Rose opened his mouth, as if to warn me from that question, but the words never left his lips, because a girl appeared, a perfectly normal looking girl with brown hair and brown eyes, not quite an adult, I thought, but close enough. She wore a t-shirt and jeans and a hat not unlike the one Sam Rose wore, but hers was not wet.

In fact, the rain did not seem to affect her at all. She folded her arms, regarded Russ with a look that I suspected told her much more than he would have wanted, and shook her head.

"Wizards are not unlike cats when it comes to curiosity," she said. "And we *all* know what happens to curious cats."

"But cats have nine lives," Russ said. "Wizards don't."

The girl smiled. "Exactly."

Sam Rose, on the other hand, seemed to be at a loss. Obviously, he'd expected the girl to react some other way, perhaps adversely. He touched the cross, almost for comfort, and glanced at me. Frowned.

The girl noticed, and her smile vanished. "You really shouldn't be here."

Russ spread his hands. "And I'll ask again: This is not a public road?"

"It used to be," the girl allowed. "But the bridge is out. Why would anyone want to come here?"

"This is not Faerie," Russ said, and took a step backwards, towards me. "So the rules of the Human Realm apply. This is a human road; a human place."

"And you *assume* I am not human," the girl said, amused.

"I used to hunt vampires for a living," Russ said. "So, yes, I assume you're not human."

"You are the sorcerer Russell Moore," the girl said, abruptly. "I know you now." She glared at me--not that I had spoken--then transferred her fury to Sam Rose, who would have responded, I thought, but the sun broke free of the clouds and he faded away. The girl walked to the edge of the driveway and stood there with her toes right on the line; a line, I realized a moment later, that she could not cross.

Russ seemed to realize the same thing; he smiled, slightly, and gave her a little bow. "I am."

"What must I do to get you to leave?"

"Convince me you're not holding Mr. Rose against his will," Russ said softly, and the girl drew herself upright, her eyes narrowed, her lips pressed thin. She cast out her hand and Sam Rose appeared--in sunlight--both hands upraised as if he intended to ward us off, or ward the girl off, since she turned on him.

"Sam, am I holding you here against your will?"

Sam Rose folded his arms. He glanced at me, then at Russ, then at the girl. "How do you expect me to answer that question?"

"With the truth!" She shouted this, and the driveway behind her; in fact, the entire forest shimmered and faded with her fury.

Russ grabbed at my hand without taking his gaze from the girl. And I felt him tremble as I stepped up next to him and took his arm. He leaned on me without seeming to lean on me, and I wondered what would happen if he collapsed. If the girl couldn't pass beyond the edge of the driveway, I thought we would be safe, but Sam Rose didn't have that problem.

"I can't answer that question," Sam Rose said, his voice soft. "Because I don't know."

The girl opened her mouth to reply, then closed it. "Very well," she finally said, and quite suddenly, she seemed less a girl and more a creature to be reckoned with; even her clothing changed, subtly, although the hat remained. "Shall I release you to your grave? Is that what you want? Or perhaps I should leave you for the sorcerer to sort out; he seems to be good at that sort of thing."

"There is no need for that," Russ said quickly.

The girl transferred her gaze to him. "You are *not* well." She stalked to the edge of the driveway again, and peered at him, her hands clenched. "Why would you court my anger when you cannot protect yourself or your lady? I could destroy you!"

"Could you really?" I asked before I could stop myself.

The girl spread her hands apart, considering. "If I tried, he would attempt to stop me, and he would die, not necessarily by my hand. You were here earlier, and you left; why did you come back?"

"Curiosity," I admitted, and the girl laughed.

"I do not hold him against his will," she said. "He is bound here; as am I. Is it my *fault* he is bound here? Perhaps. Can I release him? No more than I can release myself. Does that answer your questions?"

"Who bound *you?*" Sam Rose asked, sounding as if this was all new to him.

"You said 'one of those' who live here, before," Russ said. "Are there more of you?"

"No more," the girl said. "Just me. And if you discover the wizard who bound me here, please let me know, because I would like his head. *Detached* from his body, preferably."

"How long ago was this?" I asked, thinking of Kyren and Beth, and how long memories seemed to be when it came to magic.

"I don't know," the girl said. "Long enough. That bridge was intact, the tree beside the creek only a sapling."

The tree beside the creek was an oak, and large enough to wrap my arms around. I wasn't sure how old that meant it was, but I bet I could find the answer in a book or online. "And how long have *you* been here?" I asked Sam Rose.

He hesitated. Glanced at the girl. "What year is it?"

Russ told him, simply. And he closed his eyes. "Twenty-eight years, then."

"And you never asked if she is keeping you here?" I asked, then realized what my question had to sound like to someone who had just discovered he'd been trapped in a place for twenty-eight years.

"I...I assumed that I drowned," Sam Rose said, his voice soft. "And that I was trapped here. A ghost."

Throughout this, the girl remained silent, her gaze on Russ, not Sam or me.

"Ghosts usually can't affect their surroundings," I said. "You can."

"But only when it's raining," Sam said, and then glanced up at the sun. "Except for now."

"I could have helped with that," the girl said, her voice small. "I'm sorry. I...I was used to being alone when you came. I don't think I was very nice to you."

From the expression on Sam's face, her words only brushed the surface of how she had treated him, but he'd either accepted the fact that they were trapped together or he'd forgiven her over the years.

"What is your name?" Russ asked.

"You may call me Annabelle," the girl said.

"That was my mother's name," Sam said slowly, and the girl flushed.

I wondered what she was, this girl, who--alternately--seemed to be innocent and knowing. Was she dangerous? Had *she* trapped Sam, or were they truly both trapped together?

Russ seemed to have the same sorts of questions. "Why were you trapped here?" he asked the girl, who stepped back at his regard. "Was it something you did, or was it on the wizard's whim?"

"I am innocent," the girl said, but she spoke in a way that made me wonder if she truly was innocent.

"How old were you when you wrecked your car?" Russ asked, and when Sam opened his mouth to reply, the girl screamed.

"Cover your ears!" Russ shouted, and darted forward; as I tried to obey, he grabbed Sam Rose's arm and pulled him backwards, away from the cross; away from the girl, who kept screaming, her face both bright and terrible to behold. The sound was almost as bad as a banshee's scream; covering my ears did not really help. And Russ hadn't covered his ears at all; he turned, with Sam Rose still in tow, and took two steps towards me before he collapsed.

Sam caught him. Lifted him up and with a questioning glance at me, half-carried Russ to the car, shoved him inside, and then, as I scurried around to the driver's side door, he stepped back and closed the door.

"Get in," I said over the awful sound of her screaming.

He hesitated.

"Get in," I repeated, not knowing if he *could;* not knowing if it would work.

He didn't speak, just opened the door and slid into the passenger side seat, stiff and staring, his eyes wide.

I waited until he'd closed the door and then I started to back the car the way we came--and I'm *terrible* at backing up, so I didn't dare take my eyes off the mirrors or the road.

Only when I saw the main road behind me, and the flashing light of the detour signs, did I realize that Sam Rose had vanished. Not in a whiff of smoke or anything like that; he'd merely faded away like the stories of the vanishing hitchhiker.

I almost went back for him, but Russ lay unconscious in the back of my car, and I had no way of combating the girl--Annabelle, or whoever she was. I had no idea of her origins, or the reasons behind her exile at the end of a forgotten road.

So I drove back to Russ' house, so there wouldn't be any questions as to why I had to practically carry him inside, and I settled him down on the couch, called Sennet, made tea, and waited for him to wake up.

Sam Rose would have to wait.

Chapter 3

"What has he told you?" Sennet asked an hour later as we sat at Russ' kitchen table, which had, like everything else in the house, probably come out of Lucas' basement.

"I doubt he told me everything," I said. "He really didn't have a chance. He told me he can't eat, and that he's not supposed to use magic for the next week and a half--" I hesitated. "He also said that you said that this wasn't fatal."

"Fatal, no," Sennet said. "Potentially chronic, yes." She glanced back at the hallway, as if gauging how much she should say before Russ woke up. "I didn't know about the not eating."

"He didn't tell me what he *could* eat," I said. "And this...this wasn't his fault." As succinctly as I could, I explained about the girl, and the detour, and Sam Rose. "It's my fault. If we'd come right back here, he'd be okay."

"You can feel guilty or you can do something about it," Sennet said. "It's never a good thing to dwell on guilt. And he's an adult. He can make his own decisions."

"But he'll be okay?" I asked.

Sennet hesitated. "I can't guarantee he'll recover from this completely. He told you about the 'restorative'; it's a bit more complicated than that. He *existed* on it. Comparing it to heroin is not a bad idea, but it's probably worse. That serum he used? He halfway made himself into a vampire."

"How do you *halfway* make yourself into a vampire?" I asked, realizing as I spoke that I probably didn't want to know.

"That's something you'll have to ask him," Sennet said. "Because I'm not sure I understand it myself. What has he been eating?"

"Vegetarian," I said, realizing that was probably not a good thing. I rose, opened the fridge, and stared at the contents: a carton of soy milk, orange juice way past its prime, and a hunk of cheese covered with mold. The pantry was no better; what he didn't have in junk food he made up with canned fruits and vegetables. That made me feel a *little* better; at least he had some food in the house.

"He needs to eat meat," Sennet said. "He has to substitute what he got from his 'restorative' with *something;* otherwise he'll starve to death. And not chicken or fish. *Red* meat. Preferably rare."

"He doesn't eat meat," I said.

"He needs to," Sennet replied. "It's not an option."

"Then I'll grocery shop for him," I said, and wondered if I could make him see reason. "And I'll make sure he eats."

"Someone needs to," Sennet said. "Because it's quite obvious he can't do it by himself."

I felt guilty anew at her words, because I had let him go. I hadn't protested when he moved out; hadn't inquired about his eating habits; had assumed everything was fine because he hadn't said one word or asked for help.

Until now.

"Will you mind staying here while I run to the store?" I asked, already composing a list in my mind.

"Go," Sennet said. "I'll stay." She hesitated again. "You might want to pick up organic meat; free-range or whatever you can find. I think he'd have less of an objection to that."

"That might take me a little longer," I warned, because the local grocery store didn't carry many organic products.

"He won't wake up until the sun sets," Sennet said.

And true to her word, he did not.

I'd been back for an hour and a half by the time he appeared in the kitchen doorway, tousled from sleep and the rain, his hair a rat's nest of curly tangles; the shadows under his eyes deep enough to drown in.

He stood there for a moment, staring at me, blinking in the light. And then, in a whisper, he asked, "What are you cooking?"

"Steak," I said. "Healer's orders."

"Sennet was here," Russ said, and sighed. "I don't eat--"

"Grass fed and grass *finished*," I told him. "And local, too. It cost me twenty bucks a pound, and I hope it tastes as good as it smells."

Russ was silent, staring at the skillet I'd brought back with me.

"Would you eat it? Please?" I asked. "For me? Just to see if it helps?"

"Sennet thinks it would?" Russ asked with faint hope.

"Yes," I said. "She does. She also thinks you're way too stubborn. And she doesn't want you to starve to death."

After another long moment of silence, Russ said, "Yes. I'll eat it for you."

I'd cooked his steak as rare as I dared, and he turned a little green the first time he cut into it, but he closed his eyes, and popped it in his mouth, and chewed, and then...almost automatically, he ate the whole thing, piece by piece. And half of mine, because I'd fixed myself vegetables to go with my dinner, and he didn't even ask for a bite of them, not once.

And when he was finished, we sat for a few minutes, and he drank a cup of mint tea. Without protest, which surprised me, because he usually insisted on coffee. And we waited, and when nothing happened, he opened his eyes wide and he stared at me, almost fearful. "What happened? Back at the detour?"

"What do you remember?" I asked.

"I remember asking Sam Rose how old he was when he wrecked his car," Russ said, musing, his eyes clearer than they had been in weeks. "And the girl--Annabelle--started screaming."

I told him the rest of it, and he nodded, and stared off into space with a thoughtful look on his face. "There's something odd going on. He shouldn't have been able to touch either of us if he is really a ghost."

"Well, he's going to have to keep," I said. "Because you're not going back there, at least not right now, and neither am I."

Russ looked briefly mutinous.

I folded my arms. "You collapsed," I told him. "What if she had attacked? I had no way to protect you. If Sam hadn't grabbed you, you might have fallen right inside the line she couldn't cross, and then what might have happened?"

He closed his eyes and rubbed the bridge of his nose. "You're right." His voice was very soft. "I'm sorry."

"You have nothing to be sorry about," I said firmly. "It was *my* fault, not yours. We didn't have to go at all."

Russ looked as if he wanted to argue, but he stopped the words before they could leave his mouth. He motioned to his plate. "Then...all of this?"

"I want you to be well," I said. "I want you to be happy."

"But you knew I don't eat meat," Russ said. "Did Sennet--"

"How do you feel?" I asked.

He hesitated. Then, grudgingly, "Actually, much better. You're going to think I'm stupid..."

"No."

"I didn't believe her when she told me," he said, as if I hadn't spoken. "I thought I could get through this without...without killing anything else."

"Plants die when you eat them, too," I said.

"That's not what I--"

"At least this way, you're supporting a local business and you know the animal lived a good life," I said, and he stared at me unhappily.

"I made a vow," he finally said.

"To your wife, and daughter," I guessed, because he was--almost to a fault--exceedingly loyal.

"Right after I was captured by the Kentucky vampires," Russ whispered. "When they released me. Before Naomi took Rosemarie and left. I promised her that things would be different. She..."

There were tears, of course, streaming down his cheeks, but he made no move to wipe them away.

"Where are they buried?" I asked.

Russ blinked. "They're buried in a little cemetery outside of Columbus."

"Are you up for a road trip?" I asked, and glanced at the clock. It was ten o'clock; it would take us almost two hours to get to Columbus anyway.

"What?"

"We could be at the cemetery by midnight," I said, and then, when he didn't respond, "the witching hour."

"I have my doubts that Naomi and Rosemarie would come back as ghosts," Russ said, but he sounded uncertain.

"Is it worth a try?" I asked. "To ask forgiveness? And permission to break your vow?"

"I've already broken it," he whispered, and indicated his plate.

I just stared at him, waiting, because we both knew that wasn't necessarily true. And he stared back at me, and then, softly, he whispered, "Yes."

"This has to be your decision," I said gently. "I'll drive you there, I'll drive you back, but you have to decide if this is something you can live with."

"You're not...you're not going to force me to--" He struggled for the words he wanted to say, but I already knew them. And I realized I was walking a fine line now; if he decided he couldn't live with what he'd done to himself, then I would have to allow him the dignity of a choice, no matter how hard it was.

And I would have to defend his choice.

"No," I said. "I'm not going to force anything on you. You're an adult. You can make your own decisions. Don't get me wrong--I hope you decide you'd like to stay here..." I faltered, then pushed on. "With me, but I..."

Russ smiled. It was a wholly joyful smile, almost kin to the one he'd worn when he appeared outside of Ivy's door. The first time I'd ever seen him. I felt my eyes fill with tears I did not want to shed.

"I would like to stay here," he said, deliberately enunciating every word. "With you." Now it was his turn to hesitate. "But you're right. I should...there's something I have to do first. And if you don't mind driving--"

"Of course not," I said.

"You might not be back in time to go to work tomorrow," Russ warned.

"The library can live without me for one more day," I said softly. "I'm not sure you could."

"I'm not sure I could have either," Russ said. And then, "Thank you."

We left the dishes on the table; the skillet unwashed. I didn't want him to change his mind if we stopped to clean up. Once we were in my car, he gave me terse directions, then huddled in his seat, silent.

It was an hour before he spoke again. "I blamed myself, you know."

"I know," I said.

"We weren't angry with each other. We were going to work things out. Later on, I found out that Andre got into the house by telling her I was dead." His voice was steady, but soft, almost blending in with the sound of my car's tires against the pavement. "I found them, later; Andre called me and told me what he had done."

"I'm sorry," I said, even though I knew it wouldn't help. He'd had no chance to mourn them; no chance to get past the crushing grief.

"I didn't go to the funeral," Russ whispered. "I was on the run by then."

If we arrived at the cemetery by midnight and nothing happened, then I'd have to assume their souls were at rest. Otherwise, if they appeared, maybe Russ would walk away with some sense of closure.

"You're not on the run anymore," I said, and he laughed, although his laugh was closer to a sob.

"That's true." He glanced at me. "Can I drive for a bit?"

"Are you *allowed* to drive?" I asked.

"Just not my van," he said. "And it would give me something to do with my mind."

Other than to dwell on what could have been, I thought, but didn't say that aloud. "Sure. You can drive."

I pulled over into the next rest area, and we switched seats. And an hour after that, we arrived at our destination; a small, sleepy cemetery outside of an equally sleepy town.

The only problem I could foresee was that the local law enforcement would wonder what we were doing in the middle of a cemetery at midnight, but Russ had already thought of that. He pulled the car in the small parking lot and turned off both the engine and the lights.

"We'll walk from here. It will attract less attention."

"There's a flashlight in the glovebox," I said, and he took it out and switched it on.

The spring night was cool, not cold, and the recent rains had turned the ground to mush. We walked hand in hand across the muddy ground, Russ stopping here, then there, to orient himself.

And we found them, or at least their graves, finally, under a small lilac that was just getting ready to bud.

One gravestone, two names. And lines of a poem I recognized.

Russ dropped to his knees in front of the gravestone, closed his eyes, and whispered,

'Can death be sleep if life is but a dream
And dreams of bliss pass as a phantom by
The transient pleasures as a vision seem,
And yet we think the greatest pain's to die--'

"John Keats," I said when he stopped.

"Yes. It was her favorite poem."

"Then you might as well finish it," I said. "It's not quite midnight."

'How strange it is that man on earth should roam
And lead a life of woe but not forsake
His rugged path; nor dare he view alone
His future doom, which is but to awake.'

His voice drifted away on a cool breeze that smelled of winter, not spring.

I hadn't noticed the fog, at first, but it drifted now, among the gravestones, a white, unearthly mist that spread across the ground like a living thing. When it reached us, it--*avoided* us, or seemed to; it pooled around the gravestone, but left us in a small circle of clear air.

Russ didn't seem to notice. He'd bowed his head, too lost in misery to pay attention. But I touched his shoulder when faint figures appeared in the mist; far too many for me to count.

"Russ?" I whispered his name and he raised his head.

The figures--spirits, or whatever they were--drew back. A ripple of *something;* some emotion, perhaps, coursed through them, spreading far and wide, as if my speaking his name had thrown something disturbing in their midst.

Slowly, making sure each movement was deliberate and visible, Russ managed to climb to his feet. He stumbled once; I took hold of his arm, and he did not shake me off.

"I'm looking for Naomi and Rosemarie Moore," he said, and his voice only cracked at the end of the request, a small piece of grief lodged inside a name. "If they are here."

On the edge of my hearing, I heard a murmur swarm through the crowd. Not quite as loud as the wind rustling leaves; not quite as soft as the sound of a baby's breath. The crowd of spirits pushed forward, and then, abruptly, parted.

Rosemarie had been a baby still when she'd been murdered. But the child who stood pressed against her mother's legs was older; four, perhaps, and she had her mother's dark hair. But she had Russ' eyes, inquisitive and bright.

Russ stopped breathing. I don't think he realized it; he just froze in place, staring at them, his arm rock hard under my grasp as if he'd turned to stone. But when I tried to release him, he clutched at my hand as if he were drowning, and whispered, "Please stay."

I wasn't sure if he spoke to his wife and child or to me. But I did not move from his side.

"Sometimes I wish I'd believed in reincarnation," Naomi said before the silence grew too great. She had a low, musical voice; soothing and soft.

Russ sucked in a breath, then choked, coughing as his lungs strained for air. I held him upright; otherwise he would have fallen. And Naomi transferred her gaze to me.

I felt no anger from her; no sign that she minded that I stood next to Russ and she did not. Only sadness, and perhaps relief, as if she'd been waiting for him to come for far too long.

"What would have happened if you had?" Russ asked hoarsely. He couldn't stop staring at Rosemarie, who stared right back at him, both shy and curious.

"I don't know," Naomi said. "I might have come back. Rosemarie might have come back. But we wouldn't necessarily have been together." She stared at him, appraisingly. "You look terrible, Russ."

"I've been..." He struggled with everything he wanted to tell her; I felt his anxiety, his sorrow, his fear.

"I know," Naomi said, softly. "I heard. We are not as isolated as it might seem."

"Can I...can I touch you?"

"No," Naomi said. "Not until Halloween."

Halloween had many legends and myths attached to it, but I'd never heard this one. "What do you mean?" I asked.

"They died on Halloween," Russ whispered.

"On the day you die you can interact with us?" I asked. "With anyone?"

"Yes," Naomi said. "And it's doubly important for us."

"In what way?" Russ asked.

"We *age*," Naomi said, and now it made sense, the reason why Rosemarie would not be a baby forever. "Until our natural deaths."

"I don't believe in predestination," Russ said, almost sharply.

"Just because you don't believe in it doesn't mean it doesn't exist," Naomi replied, as if this was an old argument.

Russ deflated. "Yes. I know."

Surprised, Naomi laughed. "You've changed."

"It's been four years," Russ said. He glanced at me, then released my arm and took a step forward, towards Naomi and Rosemarie. And then, almost as if he had planned it, he dropped--or fell--to his knees.

And Rosemarie ventured out from behind her mother's legs; slowly walking forward until she stood just a foot away from Russ, staring at him as if she couldn't quite remember who he was. And then, she extended her hand and barely brushed the side of his face.

I wondered if Russ could feel her touch.

"Daddy?" Her little voice, so innocent, tugged at my heart. I felt my eyes fill with tears, because I couldn't help them; I couldn't go back in time to prevent what had happened four years ago. I couldn't change the past.

"No one can," Naomi said, as if she'd read my mind. "At least Andre is dead. And we *could* rest in peace."

"Only 'could'?" I asked.

"I still love him," Naomi said simply. "And I want him to be happy."

"So do I," I said, and then wondered which statement I'd replied to...or both.

Naomi nodded. "Good." She watched Rosemarie with Russ for a moment; they were whispering together and I tried not to hear what they were saying. And then, she asked, "What has he done to himself? He's skin and bones."

"He came here to ask you for absolution from his promise," I said. "That he'd never kill anything ever again to survive. Sennet said that what he did to himself was kin to halfway making himself into a vampire."

"He used to *hunt* vampires," Naomi said.

"I know."

"Sennet is a Healer," Naomi said. "Does she think he will recover?"

"She says he should," I told her. "But he has to want--"

"Ah." Naomi whispered Russ' name. When he glanced up at her, she smiled down at him. "I wish for you to live, Russell."

He opened his mouth to reply to her, then bowed his head, overcome with tears.

"Will you bring him back here on Halloween?" Naomi asked, hesitant now, as if her request was far too imposing.

"Yes, of course," I said.

She studied me for a moment, then offered me a smile. "You are a good person, Karen Montgomery," she said, even though I didn't remember giving her my name. "Will you stay with him?"

"If he wants me to stay," I said, and Russ reached out and snagged my hand. I helped him stand.

"I do," he whispered.

"I would have one request," Naomi said softly.

Months ago, my reply would have been 'anything', and I would have had to reap the consequences of that one very powerful word. But even so, my first inclination would have been to say that anyway, so I did.

Russ knew better, too. But his voice echoed after mine.

"Will you name your first child after our daughter?" Naomi asked.

I stared at her, certain she was joking. I hadn't ever really thought about children; at least, not seriously. But--

"I told you I don't believe in predestination," Russ said.

Naomi smiled. "Even so."

"Yes," I said, because it seemed the only thing I could say. "If we have a daughter, then I promise you her name will be Rosemarie."

The real Rosemarie smiled at this, and leaned over to try to tug on Russ' shirt. He leaned down, and she whispered something, and he stared at her, his face a study in shock. And then she skipped back to her mother, who took her hand.

And they faded away.

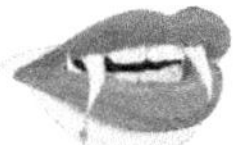

Russ remained standing long after they were gone; long after the mist had drifted off into the darkness. Long enough for me to start to wonder if he'd fallen asleep standing up, or worse.

But then, finally, he stirred, and turned, and half-fell against me. His eyes were closed. He whispered something; my name, I thought.

"You're going to have to walk," I whispered in his ear. "I can't carry you back to the car."

He roused himself with an obvious effort. "Leave me."

"Not a chance," I said, because I'd seen a figure standing at the edge of a small copse of trees; a figure wearing a *very* familiar hat.

And he approached as soon as he saw that I'd noticed him, slowly, walking across the graves, his hands empty and loose at his sides.

I stood there and waited, because Russ was unconscious again, a dead weight in my arms, and I knew I couldn't drag him back to the car without either killing myself or killing him.

"I'm not going to ask how you got here, or why you're haunting me," I said, and Sam Rose stopped a few feet away, his face in shadow again.

"I'm not haunting you," he said.

"Help me carry him back to the car," I told him, in no mood for riddles.

"I don't know if I can..." But I'd already shoved Russ at him, and he reflexively caught his arm, and then, without protest, he helped me maneuver Russ back to the car.

I made sure Russ was safely inside before turning to face Sam Rose. "You disappeared."

"Annabelle called me back," he said. "Evidently, I don't have a choice in that matter."

"And I assume she sent you here as well?"

He hesitated, then nodded. Touched my car as he had before, as if to reassure himself it was really there. "She requests your help," he said. *"His* help. And she apologizes for any harm she might have caused."

"How old *were* you when you crashed your car?" I asked, since he'd never answered that question.

Sam closed his eyes. "Eighteen."

"You look much older," I said, shocked. "Have you seen yourself lately?"

"There are *rules,* she says," Sam said, his eyes still closed. "I know I have aged."

"Are you..." There was no polite way to ask. "Are you a ghost?" At least *that* sounded better than 'Are you dead?'

"I don't know," Sam said. He touched my car again, then clenched his hands into fists. "All I know is that I can't touch everything. It used to be only in the rain. Now, it seems to be only certain things; certain people."

"Like us," I said.

He nodded. "Yes."

"Russ is in no shape to help anyone right now," I said. "But when he wakes up, I'll pass along the message." He turned to go; I reached out and touched his arm. "Did she hurt *you?*"

"No more than she ever has," Sam whispered.

"Do you want to stay with her?" I asked, even though I knew I couldn't guarantee we could free him.

He made an odd motion with his right hand, almost brushing my words away. "Do I have a choice?"

"I don't know," I said. "I wish I did."

"When you return, would you do me a favor?" Sam asked, his voice soft.

"If it's something I can do, then yes," I said, because I owed him that much for helping me with Russ.

"Could you...could you see if I died? If I'm buried somewhere?" For a moment, I saw the eighteen year old in his gaze, staring out at me through an older face. Uncertain. Scared.

Lonely.

"I work at the library," I told him. "I can find out."

He nodded, and turned away again.

"How will you get back?" I asked.

He turned, and smiled again. "I just fade away," he said, and did just that. In retrospect, my having to drive an hour and a half to get home was just not fair.

I slid into the driver's seat and glanced over at Russ, whose eyes were still closed. "Russ? Can you hear me?"

He murmured something. Frowned. But did not awaken.

"We have to stop doing this," I told him, then put my car into gear and pulled out of the parking lot.

He slept the whole way home.

Chapter 4

I woke late the next morning, stiff and aching on Russ' couch. Far too late to call in to work; the sun streamed through the window in the hallway, although it was rather dark in the living room because someone had drawn the blinds.

Someone had also made coffee; I could smell it, and the scent drew me into the kitchen where I found a mug and hot coffee waiting for me on the counter.

I poured and drank without asking questions. And by the time I was on my second cup, Russ stood in the doorway behind me...a very different Russ than the previous night.

I set down my cup.

"I called Penny at the library and told her you wouldn't be in," he said before I could speak.

I wasn't worried about my job. The library could function without me for two days. "Thank you." And then, because I was curious, I asked, "How long have you been up?"

He'd taken a shower; his hair was still damp. He was still far too thin, of course--that would take more than a night to fix--but he carried himself differently now; almost as if a weight had lifted off his shoulders.

"Since..." he glanced at the nearest clock. "Seven. I'll make you breakfast."

It was almost eleven o'clock now. My stomach growled, reminding me that I hadn't eaten since the night before. "Okay, then," I said. "Breakfast. Did *you* eat?"

"Yes. But I'll eat again with you and call it lunch." He opened the fridge, removed a dozen eggs and a stick of butter. "Pancakes? Eggs? I'll fry more bacon, too, or sausage."

"I didn't buy you any bacon or sausage," I said suspiciously, but I sat down at the table and let him work.

"Yes, I know," he said, and glanced at me. "I went grocery shopping earlier. I didn't think you'd mind if I borrowed your car."

"You must be feeling better," I said, inanely, because it was *obvious* he felt much better.

He busied himself at the stove for a few moments before replying. "Yes. I'm feeling much better."

I waited until he'd set a plate of pancakes, eggs, and bacon in front of me before asking my next question. "Better enough for magic?"

"The coffee pot has a 'keep warm' setting," Russ said mildly, and joined me with a plate of his own. Heavy on the bacon and eggs, light on the pancakes.

"Oh," I said. "Of course it does." In my defense, I am never at my best first thing in the morning.

"No magic," he said. "Sennet would be proud." He said this without a single ounce of self-pity; without a single scrap of sarcasm.

"Yes, she would be," I said. "So..."

"So."

"I never really thought of myself as the motherly type," I said, which wasn't what I wanted to say at all.

"And I still don't believe in predestination," Russ said quietly.

I stared at him. "Even after what Naomi said?"

"Even after my daughter told me that if I have another child, she might be able to come back," Russ said, and now his eyes were bright with unshed tears. "Because I *refuse* to believe that they died because of some great cosmic reason beyond my control."

"But if it ever were to happen, I'm fine with the name Rosemarie," I said.

He smiled through his tears. "I know."

"I should tell you what happened after you fainted. And I have to look something up in the newspaper archives, too."

"I thought..." For a moment, Russ looked uncertain. "I thought we could go for a walk first."

"Where?" I asked, but then I knew. "Oh. The house!"

With exaggerated care, Russ set a small ring of keys on the table in front of me. "I took the liberty of asking Lucas for the keys."

"My," I said. "You *were* busy this morning."

"Do you want to see it?" Russ asked. "If you're too tired, then we can wait; I just--"

"Of course I want to see it," I told him. "I'm a bit underdressed at the moment, though."

Russ grinned. "I assume you didn't see your overnight bag in the living room?"

"If I noticed *anything* before my first cup of coffee, it would be a miracle," I said. "What *didn't* you think of?"

"I forgot to pack your toothbrush," Russ admitted.

"Well, I'll just have to live with that," I said, and went to make myself presentable.

Forty-five minutes later, we were on our way through the forest that surrounded Russ' cottage, walking down an overgrown driveway that had to stretch at least a half mile long. The driveway was actually attached to Russ' driveway, or it *had* been, years ago, when his house was the carriage house and nothing more.

"So tell me what happened," he said. "Because I don't remember a thing after...after Naomi and Rosemarie disappeared."

I told him, as we walked, enjoying the spring sunshine and the sound of birds in the trees. And when he took my hand, it seemed the most natural thing in the world.

"I'll admit I'm very curious about Annabelle," Russ said. "And even more curious about Sam. I really don't remember reading anything about something like this, mythology-wise, I mean."

"You're welcome to come with me and help me search through the records," I said. "Some of the newspaper archives aren't online quite yet."

"Whose spare time project is that?" Russ asked.

"Technically mine," I said. "Although I'm looking to subcontract. Are you interested? It would be a perfect job for a recuperating wizard."

"You make it sound like I'm recovering from wizardry," Russ said in mock outrage, but by then we'd turned a bend, and I saw the house sitting forgotten and forlorn in the middle of what once had been a lawn, and I couldn't find enough breath for a witty reply.

It *wasn't* a mansion. It was a perfectly respectable vaguely Colonial, two rooms up, two rooms down, with an addition off the back--maybe *two* additions; I couldn't quite tell. The front part of the house had been made with local stone like Lucas' cottage, but this was no cottage. And a few early daffodils had poked up out of the ravaged flowerbeds, bravely putting on a show just for us.

I turned towards Russ. "What's the catch?"

"The house is on the National Historic Register," Russ said. "The front part was built in 1803. And the woods are in a forest conservatory; they can't be developed."

"Not a problem," I said. "What's the *real* catch? Do I have to declare undying loyalty to the Council or something?" There were no broken windows that I could see. The roof was slate; it looked to be intact. Someone had kept up the bare minimum of care; they'd let the lawn go, but the house looked to be in good shape.

"The former owner was a wizard," Russ said. "A solitary sort; he wasn't a member of the Council, but he worked with them on occasion. He also left a caveat in his will...that *he* had to approve the next owner of his house."

"Ah," I said. "I *knew* there had to be a catch. How many people have tried to buy it?"

"Lucas stopped showing it ten years ago," Russ said. "Because no one ever stayed more than a night in the house, even with the specifications."

"You have to spend the night?" I asked, and every ghost story I'd ever read rose up in my mind to haunt me.

"There are no mice," Russ said. "It's cleaned fairly regularly; always in the daytime, of course. Lucas visits from time to time."

"Are we allowed to go inside?" I asked.

Russ held up the keys. "That's what I have these for."

I followed him up the wide stone steps to the front door. He inserted the key in the lock, turned it, and the door opened without a whisper of sound.

"I'd think that if this was a *real* haunted house, the door would creak," I said.

"That comes later, or so I've been told," Russ said, and motioned me forward.

I stepped over the threshold. And something in the house--some unseen presence--took notice.

It wasn't a malevolent presence, only a curious one, and it followed us into the hallway and what would be the living room; another room could have been the parlor or a formal dining room, perhaps. The house was simply furnished, all well-worn antiques, and there were books in every single room.

A staircase led upwards, but we walked down the hall to the back of the house and the addition, which was a fairly modern kitchen with outdated appliances, yes, but nothing that couldn't be replaced, if needed. There was a breakfast nook with a small table and two chairs, more books, of course, and various other kitchen implements that were both functional and decorative.

I approved wholeheartedly, especially after I saw the dog-eared and battered copy of *The Joy of Cooking* on the cookbook shelf.

"There are two bedrooms upstairs," Russ said, glancing around the room, as if he were looking for something.

"I thought you said there was a library, too?" I asked. "Or did you just tell me that to get me to come here?"

I'd thought the kitchen was the only addition, but a door appeared--and I swear it just *appeared*--past the fridge. In any other house, it would have led to the basement. But the door to the basement was on the other wall; leading downward into the older part of the house.

With a questioning glance at Russ, I opened the door. And Russ stepped back, clearly startled. Had he not seen it appear?

"It wasn't here a minute ago," I said to assure him.

"The last time I was here, that door was in another room," he said. "Upstairs, off the smaller bedroom."

"Well, it's here now," I said. "Is there any reason why we shouldn't go inside?"

"It won't disappear, if that's what you mean," Russ said. "Lucas told me it might not even appear. Peter's very cautious of his library."

"Well, I'm a librarian," I said for the benefit of the invisible watcher. "I can certainly understand that."

When I stepped through the door, I couldn't see a thing at first; there were either no windows--a drawback, I thought--or the curtains were thick enough to shut out the sun. I felt squishy carpet, or perhaps a rug, under my feet, and the faintest scent of old leather and glue and paper.

An intoxicating scent.

"Is there a light in here, or shall we fumble around in the dark?" I asked.

"I can..." Russ began.

I knew what he was going to say. "No. You're still recuperating, remember?"

And across the room, a candle--a *bare* candle--flared into light. "Russ!"

"That wasn't me," he managed to say before I turned on him.

"And *I* can't believe that the owner of this house would allow a candle burning near these books," I replied, slightly sharper than I'd intended, because I really *did* want to get a look at them before Peter drove us out.

The candle changed into an oil lamp, and then, as if the presence realized I'd protest about that, too, it changed into one of those Tiffany-style stained glass lamps. With dragonflies.

"That will do," I said, although it was a rather ugly lamp. "Thank you."

"Who are you talking to?" Russ asked. "Peter shouldn't appear until dusk."

The invisible presence and I shared a secret, it seemed, although if Russ had been here before, I wasn't sure why it was such a secret. "He's here," I said. "I felt him as soon as we walked through the door."

"You felt..." Russ stared at me. "I must be losing my touch."

"Or maybe I'm just more attuned to ghosts," I said.

"Maybe you are," Russ murmured, and stepped aside as I approached the first bookcase.

The library was--of course--filled with books of all different subjects as a true library should be. And they weren't all ancient priceless tomes, either. Modern books fought for space on the shelves with crumbling leatherbound doorstops (not that I would *ever* use a book as a doorstop.) There were even books stacked on the massive desk that sat in the middle of the room; a dark, almost black wood--perhaps walnut--simple in style, but not in presence.

"How long were you planning on staying here?" I asked, peering at the titles on the nearest bookshelf.

Russ laughed. "As long as you want," he said. "Although if you want to look up that information in the archives..."

I pulled myself away from the bookshelf. "True. And I do want to look that up before the library closes. Shall we go upstairs?"

I let my hand drift across the nearest stack of books. They were curiously free of dust. "And then maybe we could come back later so I can look at these?" Why did I feel so bereft?

"Do you like the house?" Russ asked, and although I couldn't see his face, I thought he might be smiling.

"I love the house," I said, and meant it. "I could do without that lamp, but the house is fine. Perfect, even. Although I'd need to use one of the bedrooms for *my* library, since this one's a bit full. Which is how a library should be, honestly."

"I think the room might expand a bit for your collection," Russ murmured, and we stepped out of the room, not into the kitchen, but upstairs, I thought. Into a bedroom. The smaller one he'd mentioned?

"The moving rooms might take a bit to get used to," I said, and walked over to the window to peer outside.

The windowsills were at least a foot thick; those old stone houses were built to last. And even up here in the bedroom, everything was curiously free of dust.

I opened the wardrobe doors. It was empty, at least, no full of a dead man's clothes. There were no closets. That was one drawback about old houses.

The larger bedroom, a bathroom, and a very wide hallway that was almost large enough to be a room made up the rest of the upstairs. The woodwork, unpainted, shone softly in the sunlight. The paint seemed to be in immaculate condition.

The house was perfect. Almost *too* perfect. I narrowed my eyes and folded my arms.

"What?" Russ asked from behind me.

"How long ago did Peter die?" I asked.

"Almost twenty years ago," Russ replied. "Long before I ever got here; I never met him while he was alive."

"You would have been about seventeen years old," I said. "What were you doing when you were seventeen years old?"

We'd never discussed our respective early lives; not that I had anything to hide, but the subject had never come up. And I should have known Russ might have had skeletons in his closet--he had to have become a vampire hunter for a reason, after all.

He grew very still, staring not at me, but at the wall where a painting of a farm scene hung. And then he sighed, and touched the edge of the painting, straightening it minutely. "I killed my first vampire when I was seventeen," he said.

I stepped up behind him and touched his arm. "Can you tell me about it?" When he didn't reply, I realized how that had to have sounded. "I'm sorry. You don't have to."

"Yes, I do, especially if I want to have any sort of life with you," Russ said, his voice soft. "But I'm afraid that you'll think I'm a monster."

"Maybe you were, at one time," I said. "But I don't see any signs of you being one now."

Russ smiled tightly. "Thank you." He hesitated. Glanced at me. "I'm not going to say that the vampire I killed didn't deserve to die. At least with the way things were twenty years ago. Nowadays, the vampires would probably have stopped him before it got that bad."

"Who did he kill?" I asked.

"My sister," Russ said. "And two of her friends. And my sister's boyfriend, who was driving the car. They stopped to pick up a hitchhiker on their way home from a movie."

"How did you find out a vampire killed them?"

"My sister's friend was the target," Russ said. "She...she came back."

"Did you--" I couldn't finish either the sentence or the thought.

"No!" Russ twisted away from me and walked a couple of steps before leaning against the wall. "The vampire hunters were there by then. They found me after I--" He took a deep breath. "They found me standing over the vampire's body with a knife in my hand. I thought they were going to throw me into jail."

"Aren't you supposed to use a stake?" I asked. "Or garlic? Or something?"

"I didn't know he was a vampire," Russ said. "And evidently, there are ways to get around stakes and garlic, especially if you're a late-blooming wizard. Although they don't call what they use magic."

"I still don't see how they can do that," I said.

"It's easy," Russ said. "You start with confused, guilty kids who don't know any better, and make them believe you know everything. I became very good at it."

"*Too* good," I said, remembering Andre.

"Yeah."

"So what did they do, convince you to go into hiding?" I asked.

"I went off to college," Russ said. "And they kept in touch. What I *didn't* know was that they were setting me up; the vampire I killed had kin, and they had been looking for me."

"And they found you," I guessed. "And what happened?"

"The vampire hunters convinced me to go with them," Russ said, and just from the way he spoke, I could tell he wasn't telling me the whole story. "For my safety. I dropped off the face of the earth for a while. And they trained me."

"Is Russell Moore your real name?"

"It has been for years," Russ said. "My parents are dead now. What was left of my family has been scattered to the four winds." He tried to smile, but it didn't reach his eyes. "It seems kind of silly to try to contact what might be left of my family now."

"Do you think you might ever want to?" I asked.

"Do you think *you* might ever want to?" Russ countered, since he knew about the genealogy Ivy had created for me, and he knew I'd visited my biological parents' graves.

And that I might have relatives out there, even now.

"Probably not," I said, and he nodded, satisfied.

"What were *you* doing twenty years ago?" he asked.

"Graduating from high school," I said. "Or thereabouts. Living a perfectly normal suburban existence with no idea that magic--or Faerie, or anything else--existed."

"I didn't know either, until the vampire killed my sister," Russ said. "It was very difficult to believe, at first."

We had something else in common, then. Although, my awakening hadn't been from a talent appearing, but when Ivy informed me she was a vampire.

"How are you feeling?" I asked, because he looked exhausted again, his face drawn and pale, his eyes shadowed.

"I could rest for a bit before we go back," Russ admitted. "If that's okay with you."

"Sure," I said, and wondered why I hadn't thought to bring him something to eat or drink. "Do you want me to walk back to the house and get you something to eat?"

He started to say no; I saw the word form on his lips. But then he nodded. "Would you mind?"

"Of course not," I said. "It's not that far."

"I'll be very happy when this is over and done with," Russ said, and hesitated at the top of the stairs.

I took his arm. "Here. Lean on me." And he did, and we walked slowly down the stairs and into the living room, where I helped him to a slightly worn velveteen couch. "You'll be okay here?"

"Peter doesn't usually manifest until after dark," Russ said. He leaned back and closed his eyes.

"I'll bring you something to eat," I said. "And drink. And then you can rest back at your house while I go look up Sam Rose in the library's archives." He'd done a day's worth of errands in four hours, after all; it was no wonder he was exhausted.

"Thank you," he murmured, his eyes still closed.

I hesitated, then kissed him on the cheek. "I'll be right back."

He did not respond.

Back at his house, I found an insulated bag in one of the cabinets and filled it with anything portable I found in the fridge of the pantry. He'd bought homemade jerky from somewhere that morning; I added it to the bag along with lunchmeat, and cheese, and condiments; enough for a picnic for twelve, not just two.

It was only while looking for a thermos that I found the dusty bottle shoved in the back of a cupboard...one lonely bottle of Russ' 'restorative', half-full of his strange concoction, the sediment on the bottom thick enough to be sludge.

But...half-full?

The lid twisted off easily; I smelled something rotten, ancient, old. How could he drink this stuff? I didn't even need to sniff it to know it wasn't...it wasn't *right*.

How long ago had he stopped? *Had* he stopped? How would I know? I screwed the lid back on the bottle and placed it back on the shelf; snagged the thermos beside it and filled it with coffee. I was just about to leave again when the doorbell rang.

I left the food on the kitchen table and peeked out the nearest window. A boy--a young man, really, about sixteen--stood on the porch, his hands hooked into his belt loops, the picture of nonchalance except for the way he managed to look at everything at once; I doubt he'd missed the twitch of the curtain when I'd moved it.

His hair was a bit longer than fashion warranted, but he wasn't scruffy or unshaven. Just casual. Comfortable. And on edge.

Was he a vampire hunter, perhaps? He wasn't a vampire; he'd walked through sunlight to get to the porch.

I opened the front door, keeping the screen door closed between us. "Can I help you?"

He stared at me, shocked, and took a step backwards. "I'm sorry. I was looking for Russell Moore."

I knew Russ still had enemies. I also knew--from the little he'd told me-- that he also had friends. "Who's asking?" I asked, and wondered if I'd recognize any names that he gave me.

"Oh...my name is Niles," the boy said. "But I'm here at the behest of Ethan Walker. Russ knows who I am."

I knew the name Niles and I knew the name Ethan Walker. "The Kentucky vampires," I said, and his worried look changed into a grin.

"Yeah. Although Ethan would hasten to add that we're not the only vampires in Kentucky."

It was interesting to hear a human say 'we' in regards to vampires. But I knew there were vampire families with human members; so it made sense. "Russ seems to think you are," I said.

"'Seems to'," Niles repeated. "Then he's alive?"

Russ had not mentioned wanting to contact anyone, and I had no idea if he'd tried. And maybe he just wanted to be left alone to heal after Andre's death; he'd spent almost two months with me, after all, before Lucas had offered him the cottage.

There was a cardboard box on the floor beside Niles, and a laptop bag. I thought I saw a silhouette in the car sitting in the driveway, but I couldn't quite tell. Had he come alone?

"He's alive," I said, because all he'd have to do is ask around to find out the answer to that question.

"But something happened," Niles said. "We know...we heard a little of it, but not enough to satisfy Ethan's curiosity. I know Andre's dead, but then when Russ wouldn't answer his phone..." He stopped, then, and stared at me unhappily. "We didn't know who to call."

"My name is Karen Montgomery," I said. "Come in." I stepped back and watched as he slung the laptop bag over his shoulder and picked up the box, which clanked, muffled, like...well, bottles. "What's in the box?"

Niles hesitated. "How much do you know about Russ?"

"Not nearly as much as I thought," I said. "Is that the stuff he used to drink? His 'restorative'?"

"Used to?" Niles asked, and he sounded so...so *worried* that I folded my arms and gave him my best librarian *look*.

"Tell me," I said.

"I don't have the authority to tell you," he said, and I gave him another *look*. He wilted. "I'd have to call Ethan--"

"Tell me," I said, softer. "I'm his *friend*. I care for him. And I want to see him well."

"Okay, but you're not a wizard," he said. "You might not--"

"I'll understand enough," I told him. "Sit down." I pulled out a chair from the kitchen table and sat across from him.

He sat down. Started to speak in fits and starts, his voice low. Reluctant.

It had happened early on. After Russ' family had been murdered, he'd gone into hiding...of sorts, working with Ethan to aid other vampire houses in protecting themselves from the Hunters. It was only a matter of time before he came across a group of vampires who didn't want anything to do with him, despite Ethan's assurances.

"They, um, the head of that house was a vampire named Ruby," Niles said. "She refused to let him help ward her house, the hunters attacked, and Russ tried to save her life. She was wounded. I'm not sure exactly what happened..." He glanced at me, as if gauging my reaction to that, but I didn't comment. "He barely made it back to Ethan's house."

Obviously that meant something, but I had no idea what. "And?" I asked.

"Do you know how vampires are made?" Niles asked.

"Russ is *not* a vampire," I said, but then I remembered Sennet's words. "No, I don't know how vampires are made. My assistant is a vampire, though; if you don't want to tell me, I could ask her."

Niles stared at me, surprised. "Your assistant is a vampire?"

"Her name is Ivy. And you're stalling."

"There's a sharing of blood," Niles said. "It's a bit more complicated than that, because it's--evidently--a sharing of *minds* as well, but it's really hard to make someone into a vampire accidentally."

"Sennet told me that he made himself into a vampire *halfway*," I said slowly. "She seems to think it was the restorative that did it."

"Not exactly," Niles said. "*Ruby* did it; the restorative is the only thing keeping him alive."

"Exactly what do you mean by that?" I asked.

"The halfway thing's pretty accurate," Niles said. "If he hadn't made it to Ethan's house, he probably would have died by morning, because you just don't leave someone like that. Ethan was furious."

I thought Ethan had probably been a bit more than furious. "And what did he do?"

"He asked everyone to donate blood," Niles said, and rubbed his wrist, almost unconsciously. "And he mixed it all together with some other stuff; *I* don't even know what he put into it, and he forced Russ to drink it, and when Russ woke up, he wasn't a vampire."

"But he wasn't quite human, either, was he?" I asked.

"No." Now, Niles looked wholly unhappy. And perhaps a little peeved at Ethan for putting him on the spot.

"Then why would he stop drinking it if he--" I stopped, then, because I already knew the answer to my question. "He doesn't know, does he?"

Niles folded his arms in front of his chest. "When he woke up, he could heal vampires if he gave them his blood. Like...really *heal* them."

I remembered Elise, Ivy's friend, and what Russ had done to save her. "And the serum?"

"That came later," Niles said. "He came up with that himself. He said it worked faster that way."

"But it also drained him faster," I said. "And made him pretty useless to those he was trying to save." I realized I was angry; at him, at the unseen presence of Ethan; at Russ himself.

Niles raised both hands. "Don't shoot the messenger," he said. "Ethan sent me to find him because he feared Russ was dead."

"He's not dead," I said, and realized that I needed to get back to the house before Russ awoke and found me gone and did something unwise, like try to find me with his talent. "But he's also not well. He hasn't drunk any of that stuff for three months--"

"He had to drink *some*," Niles argued. "Or else he would be dead."

I remembered the bottle in the cupboard. "I know he didn't have any bottles left in his van--at least, not where he kept them--when Andre died. He didn't drink *anything* except for coffee the first couple of weeks; he barely *spoke* to anyone. I don't know what he was drinking when he moved out of my apartment. I know when I came here yesterday, he barely had enough food to feed a mouse. And he'd been eating vegetarian."

"Is he here?" Niles asked softly.

"No." I stared at him for a moment, then decided to trust him, at least for now. "We were visiting a house I'm looking at, to buy, that is. It's about a half mile hike back in the woods. I came back here to get him something to eat."

"Can I come back with you?" Niles asked, just as I expected.

"You never answered my question," I said.

"Which one?" Niles asked, but I thought he knew anyway.

"Does he know?" I asked again.

Niles sighed. "This would be much better coming from Ethan."

"Then call him up. Tell him to start driving at dusk and we'll be here waiting," I said, a trifle sharply.

"You don't know a lot about vampires, do you?" Niles asked.

"I know more than most people," I replied. "What is it, a territorial thing?"

Niles lips quirked. "Yeah. A bit. Pretend the various vampire houses are kingdoms, and add a large dose of paranoia. If I petitioned the closest house, we might be able to *fly* him in, but driving he'd cross too many territories and the logistics would be a nightmare."

"Hence the reason why vampires have humans in their houses?" I asked. "What about those vampires who aren't members of houses?"

"Not 'members'," Niles said. "More like...cousins, I guess. Family."

"Like the mob," I said.

"Well." Niles couldn't help but laugh. "Kind of. Yes."

"Vampires don't go on vacation much, I imagine?"

"Not without a lot of paperwork," Niles said, and hesitated. "No. Ethan didn't tell him."

"Wasn't that a little cruel?" I asked.

"It's not my place to ask," Niles said, almost challenging me to say something in reply to that.

"I'd think that even Ethan would want you to have your own opinions," I said. "And I doubt he would have completely ignored your counsel."

"He still feels guilty about Russ' family," Niles said. "Russ is a sore point when it comes to opinions, and Ethan."

"And when did he intend to tell him?" I asked. "Never?"

"I don't know," Niles said. "I can't answer that. I'm not Ethan."

"But you represent him," I pointed out. "Don't you?"

Niles was silent for a moment, considering my words. "I guess I never thought about it quite like that," he said. "I've always...I've always been with someone else. This is the first time I've come alone."

"Who managed the deliveries, before?" I asked. At his blank look, I indicated the box. "How many times have you given Ethan blood for Russ?"

"We alternate," Niles said. "Every third month or so."

"For how long?" I asked.

"Three years," Niles said softly, and rubbed his wrist again.

"And how long do you intend to keep this up?"

Niles didn't reply at first. He started to answer, but the trill of a phone interrupted his words. He dug a cell phone out of a pocket of his jacket, glanced at the number, then opened it with an apologetic glance at me.

"Well, it depends on your definition of 'good news'," he said in reply to a question. "He's not dead, but I haven't seen him yet."

I thought I heard the person on the other end say my name.

"Actually, I'm sitting across from her right now," Niles said. "I'm way ahead of you." He listened for a moment, frowned, then asked me, "He wants to know if it's true that the director of your library is a dragon."

"It's true," I said. "Let me talk to him."

Wordlessly, Niles held out his phone. I put it to my ear and Ethan said, "I was under the impression that it was difficult for dragons to hold jobs in the human world."

"Not if the books in the library are her hoard," I said. He *sounded* perfectly pleasant. "The rare books with gold leaf on the pages do end up in her office most of the time, but I'm not complaining."

"Hmm. You must live in an interesting town."

"You're welcome to come and visit, I'm sure," I said.

Ethan laughed. "I doubt that, although I'd love to. The logistics--"

"Would be a nightmare, yes," I interrupted him, and Niles hid a smile. "However, I think the truth would be best coming from you and not Niles." I told him what had happened, and what Russ had done. And he was silent for so long after I finished speaking that I had half-decided he had hung up on me.

"All right."

"All right?" I echoed, and Niles sat up in his chair, his eyes wide.

"I'll come." There was no laughter in Ethan's voice now.

"But I thought...Niles said--" I was flabbergasted that he'd agreed to come so quickly; and why? Did he fear Russ would die? Or worse, was he afraid that something would happen?

"I'll have to call in a couple of favors," Ethan said. "I'll need somewhere to stay, though; do you think you could ask Niles--"

"We'll take care of it," I told him. "I have a spare bedroom, if it comes down to that."

Ethan was momentarily silent. "You *do* know I'm a vampire, right?"

"Yes," I said. "Is there any reason why you shouldn't stay in my spare bedroom?"

"Of course not, but--"

"Then don't worry about it," I said, and wondered what Ivy would say when I told her what I had done.

"I'll be there before dawn tomorrow," Ethan said. "I promise you that. May I speak with Niles?"

Whatever he said to Niles must have been just as startling; Niles spoke only a couple of words, clearly stunned. When he hung up the phone, he stared at me, then slowly shook his head.

"I don't know what to say."

"Actually, if you don't mind doing me a favor, I'll go gather Russ and bring him back here," I said, and explained what I needed from the library archives. "It shouldn't take you more than an hour. Tell them I sent you." I had a promise to keep, after all. "Is it supposed to rain tonight?"

"I don't know," Niles said. "Shall I find out for you?"

"If you don't mind," I replied. "Although I don't know if it really matters anymore."

Niles glanced at me curiously. "There's something else going on, isn't there?"

"You could say that," I said. "And I'll tell you about it later. Come back here when you're finished, even if you don't find out anything. Okay? Did you eat lunch?"

"Yes to both questions," Niles said. "And I have money to make copies of whatever I find." He stood, left the cardboard box on the table, and slung the laptop case over his shoulder.

"And Niles...if you see a detour sign, don't try to get around it. Just go the route."

The question was on his lips, but he didn't ask it. Instead, he nodded. "I'll come right back here."

I waited until he'd pulled out, then grabbed what I had packed. Hesitated over the box, and remembered what Niles had said. In the end, I opened it, slipped a corked bottle into my bag, and hiked the overgrown driveway back to the stone house. Halfway there, I convinced myself that I'd arrive to find Russ dead; I burst into the living room with my heart in my throat, only to find him still asleep on the couch, curled onto his side.

I didn't even notice the presence of someone behind me until he spoke. "There is something terribly wrong with your friend, there."

"That's what everyone keeps telling me," I said, and turned around. An elderly man stood behind me, in the shadows of the hall, one hand clutching a cane I'd noticed in a topless wooden churn right inside the door. "Peter, I presume?"

"And you are Karen," the man inclined his head. "I wish we could have met in better circumstances."

"So do I," I said. "I adore your house."

"So did I," Peter said, and placed one hand against the nearest wall. Interestingly enough, his hand didn't pass through the wall; it rested there, as if on the shoulder of an old friend.

I knelt beside the couch with my supplies and gently shook Russ' shoulder. He did not respond. "Russ?"

"You know that he's dying," Peter said, almost hesitantly, as if dying was so terrible a thing to someone who had already died.

I didn't want to hear it. My eyes filled with tears. "Russ?"

"What did he do to himself?" Peter asked.

"It's a long story," I said, but I found myself telling him anyway, at least what I had known and what I now knew. "Ethan's coming here to tell him."

"Did you bring some of the potion?" Peter asked.

"I...yes," I admitted. "But he'll get mad at me if I--"

"Would you rather he be angry or dead?" Peter asked. "It isn't likely that he'll notice at first anyway; he's too far gone that only stubbornness has kept him alive until now. He's worn himself out. One drink will not heal him, but it will keep him alive, and mobile, until Ethan comes."

I stared at him, then at Russ, and made up my mind. "Do you have a corkscrew?"

"In the kitchen," Peter said. "I'd get it for you myself, but the only things I can touch now are my books."

"And the house," I said.

"Yes," Peter replied. "The house and I are old friends."

"I think it would be wonderful to have a house for a friend," I said, and meant every word.

"I imagine you would think that," Peter said, and faded away.

I did find a corkscrew in the kitchen, and the stuff in the bottle, although still revolting, smelled a lot better than the bottle I'd found in Russ' cupboard. I poured some of it into a juice glass, levered Russ up, and tried not to feel as if I were poisoning him when I touched the glass to his lips.

He drank without any prompting, although he frowned at the taste, his forehead furrowing into lines. But some part of his body must have realized that he needed Ethan's potion to live, because he did not turn his head away. He did not refuse it.

By the time I filled up the glass for the fourth time--the bottle was almost empty--Russ was awake. Awake, but not quite aware until he realized what he was drinking, and he stared at me, confused, and then reached out...to wipe the tears from my cheeks.

I think his first inclination was to knock the glass out of my hand, but something stopped him.

"That is not from the bottle I had in my cupboard," he whispered.

"No, it's from Niles," I said. "Ethan's on his way, or he will be. He has something to tell you."

Russ closed his eyes. Let his head fall back against the cushion. "Ethan's coming *here?*"

"Yes."

"Then I think I already know," he whispered. "Do *you* know?"

"I know what Niles told me," I hedged. "I also think it would be better coming from Ethan. He could explain--"

"Tell me." Russ said. "Please."

I told him. And he lay there for a moment with his arm over his eyes, and then he asked, "Do I smell coffee?"

"I'll pour you some," I said, and helped him sit up a moment later to drink it. And he hunched over the mug in his hands and inhaled the steam, with his eyes closed for a moment, before speaking.

"I drank some of what you found in the cupboard when I woke up this morning," Russ whispered. "Only a little bit; I wanted to see if it would stop the...the craving."

"The craving," I repeated. "Like...like for blood?"

He shivered, and almost dumped his cup. "Yes."

"Oh," I said, because I couldn't think of anything else to say.

Russ opened his eyes and smiled at me. "The steak helped."

"Just not enough," I said, understanding.

"Yes." He sipped his coffee, frowned, then asked, "Ethan's coming *here?*"

"He said he'd have to call in a few favors," I told him. "I sent Niles to look up Sam Rose's obituary--if there is one--at the library."

"You've been busy," Russ said.

I sat down next to him. "I was worried about you."

He reached out and took my hand. Brought it to his lips, and kissed it. "How long did say you thought it would take Niles to look up the information?"

"An hour or so," I said, and felt a quiver in my stomach.

"Do you still feel the presence here?" Russ asked softly.

"No," I replied. "I think Peter left. We had a conversation about you; he's the one who convinced me--"

"You had a conversation about *me*?" Russ asked, still holding my hand. He turned towards me, his eyes alight again, free from shadows.

I saw nothing inhuman in his gaze; nothing odd or unsettling. Just Russ. "Yes. He called the house his friend."

My voice must have sounded a bit wistful, because Russ laughed softly.

"Maybe it will become *your* friend, too," he said, and tucked an errant strand of hair behind my ear.

I reached out and placed my hand flat on the wall behind me, like Peter had done. I felt nothing but wall; plaster and paint and a slight warmth from the sun. "Maybe," I said. "I would like that."

"So would I," Russ replied. He hesitated. "Karen--"

"Hush," I told him. "Niles won't be back for a while. We have plenty of time. Tell me the truth. Are you going to be okay with this?"

"Yes," Russ said. "I think so. As long as you don't mind..."

I kissed him then, just to shut him up.

"I take it you don't mind," he whispered when we came up for air.

"Not a bit," I said, and although it wasn't really a two-person couch, we managed to make it work.

Much more than an hour later, we arrived back at Russ' house to find Niles waiting for us, a small stack of paper on the kitchen table the evidence of his toils. I'm not sure what he saw when he looked at us, but he gave Russ a sharp look, and then, slowly, said, "You look terrible."

"I look better than I did earlier today," Russ said, and sank down in a chair, because the walk back had been harder than I thought it would be for him. "Karen told me--"

Niles looked inordinately relieved. He started to speak, but Russ interrupted him.

"She told me, but I have a few questions. She also told me that Ethan was coming here?"

"He'd be the best person to answer any questions," Niles said. "But I'm not sure he can answer what I think you're going to ask."

"If I die, will I come back as a vampire?" Russ asked, almost sharply.

"I don't know," Niles said unhappily. "I don't think Ethan knows either. This has never been *done* before. I'm sorry. I don't know." He paused. Pushed the stack of papers towards me. "I'm glad you're not dead."

"So am I," Russ said, distantly. "So am I." He deflated a little, then, and leaned his elbows on the table so he could rest his head in his hands. "You brought more for me to drink?"

"Twelve bottles," Niles said.

"Eleven now," I replied. "He drank one. You never did answer my question, Niles."

"Which one was that?" Niles asked.

"How long are you intending to do this?" I asked, and Russ raised his head, suddenly interested. "Or is that an Ethan answer, too?"

"You know it is," Niles replied, his voice soft. "Do you need more to drink, Russ?"

"No," Russ said after a moment. "Not now. Food would be nice, though. Is there any more of that steak?"

My heart broke for a moment; a sharp twinge of sadness that he hadn't asked for this; that he'd only been trying to help. And, in all honesty, so had Ethan. "I think there's some left," I said, and left them staring at each other as I went to check.

We had a late lunch. Niles wandered outside after a bit to sit on the porch, giving us some time alone, which I appreciated. Russ ate, took a nap, then woke up to eat again and drink some more of Ethan's concoction. I tried not to worry when he fell back asleep.

Instead, I busied myself with what Niles had found in the library's archives. Two articles, one obituary, a couple of grainy pictures; Sam Rose's body had *not* been recovered, at least according to the paper.

"I searched a year out," Niles said from the doorway. "I thought that would be long enough. What's going on with that?"

He seemed subdued; tired. I motioned for him to sit down.

"Do you want anything to eat? Drink? I don't have any clue if you're old enough to drink, but--"

That brought a smile to his face. "I'm eighteen. But thanks. I'm fine. I had some water in the car."

"Sit down," I said, and he sat this time, fiddling with the pen I'd been writing with. "It's not a very long story. I got lost trying to outwit a detour two days ago and I met a ghost, or someone who seemed as if he were a ghost." I told him about Annabelle, and Sam Rose, and what had happened in the cemetery. Not about Naomi and Rosemarie; that was Russ' tale to tell, not mine.

"So Sam Rose is the ghost?" Niles asked, brightening up a bit. "Or the maybe-ghost? And Annabelle is the cipher?"

"Is Annabelle keeping him there against his will?" I asked. "Is he really dead? He's aged, he looks a lot older than me."

"You don't look very old," Niles said, then flushed.

I laughed. "I'm actually a year younger than Russ."

"So what are you planning to do?" Niles asked. "Just give him this information? Or try to figure out why he's there and who trapped Annabelle in the first place?"

"I think your second question depends on Annabelle," I said. "She wasn't very open to questions the first time. But I *am* planning to give Sam the information. I promised him I'd look it up."

"And you wanted to know if it was supposed to rain because you're not sure if he can show himself, even though he has before?" Niles asked. "You're taking a whole lot on faith."

"What do you mean?" I asked.

"Well, what if they're both working together?" Niles asked. "What if they *want* you to free them, and it's something you shouldn't do? And since he appeared to you elsewhere--in the cemetery--why doesn't he come *here* for the information, since he seems to know where to find you?"

"I think he was tracking Russ, not me," I said, but I wasn't certain of that. "Even so, what if what you're saying *isn't* true? What if they're both stuck there without cause? Even *with* cause, that's a lousy way to spend the rest of your life."

Niles smiled. "I see what Russ sees in you," he said.

I stared at him. "What?"

"You both like to fight injustice," Niles said. "Even when Russ was a vampire hunter, I've heard he always fought fair."

"How can you fight fair and be a vampire hunter?" I asked.

"You'd be surprised," Russ said from the doorway. He yawned. "Were you talking about me?"

He seemed tired, still, but much more awake than before. And he showed no sign of weakness when he poured himself a cup of coffee and joined us at the table.

"You and Karen," Niles said. "Annabelle and Sam Rose."

"Ah," Russ said. "What did you find out?"

I brought him up to date, Niles explained his concerns, and Russ listened to us both without interrupting.

"You have a good point," he said to Niles. "But I still think Karen's right; we can't *not* get to the bottom of this."

"You're both also too curious for your own good," Niles said.

Russ smiled, but didn't comment. "When will Ethan get here?"

It was still light outside, of course, but late in the afternoon now. Almost sunset. And Russ seemed more awake, more aware. Did the sun have anything to do with it?

"He called an hour ago, and said he was leaving at sunset," Niles said. "It will take him..well, it took *me* six hours to get here. It will probably take him seven."

"Is he coming alone?" Russ asked.

"He didn't say," Niles said. "Aden can't travel this far if that's why you're asking."

"Why not?" I asked.

Niles hesitated. Glanced at Russ, as if he should know the answer.

"Why not?" Russ asked. "I...I haven't talked to him in a few months, but the last time I did, he seemed to be okay--"

"He didn't tell you," Niles said, flatly.

Russ glanced at me, then back at Niles, clearly flummoxed. "No."

Niles dug his cell phone out from his pocket and laid it in front of Russ. "Call him. I'm getting tired of being the messenger."

Russ stared at the phone as if it were a bomb, his face pale and tinged with gray. But he picked up the phone and he dialed a number, and when no one picked up, he gave Niles a questioning glance.

"Who is Aden?" I asked.

"A wizard and a friend," Russ said softly, and closed the phone. "An enemy before that, though. He was on the vampires' side, I was on the hunters' side. There was a fight. My partner died; Aden ended up in a wheelchair. I didn't know he was alive until Ethan kidnapped me. Does this have anything to do with what I did to him?"

Niles pinched the bridge of his nose and briefly closed his eyes. He held out his hand for the phone, pressed a button, and put the phone up to his ear. "Is Aden with you?" he asked as soon as Ethan picked up. Ethan must have responded in the affirmative, because Niles pressed another button and set the phone in the middle of the table. "You're on speakerphone," he said. "Both Russ and Karen are here."

There was a short silence, and then Ethan asked, "Was that necessary?"

"I'm getting tired of being the messenger," Niles said shortly, and pushed back his chair.

"Please don't leave," Ethan said from the phone. Niles hesitated. He started to speak, then shook his head and walked out anyway, slamming the door behind him.

"He's angry," Ethan said into the silence.

"Why?" Russ asked. And then, when Ethan didn't reply, he said, "I know what you did. Niles told Karen. Karen told me." There was no blame in his voice.

Ethan let out a breath. "Okay. I'm glad. But I'm still coming." And then, hesitant, "Did you drink--"

"Yes," Russ said.

"Good."

There was a beeping sound behind Ethan, and a voice, on a speaker overhead.

"Where *are* you?" Russ asked.

Just as I said with sudden understanding, "You're in a hospital. Aden's in the hospital?"

"Aden is--" Ethan's voice trailed away, and a new voice took its place.

"Dying," Aden said. He sounded exhausted. "Complications from the...the accident."

"And you're not going to allow Ethan to make you into a vampire?" Russ asked.

"And be...in a wheelchair forever?" Aden whispered, slurring his words a little. "No thanks."

Russ straightened up. "You forget. My blood *heals* vampires."

"Even ones with pre-existing conditions?" It was Ethan's voice now, stronger, forceful. As if daring Russ to deny it.

"I don't know," Russ said. "But I'm willing to try. Is he? Are you?"

"Can he be moved?" I asked. "Aren't there any Healers there?"

"Aden?" Ethan's voice was muffled, as if he'd moved away from the phone. I heard Aden reply, but I couldn't make out his words. Ethan said something else; Russ closed his eyes and leaned his head in his hands.

After what seemed like an eternity, Ethan returned to the phone. "To answer your question, no. There aren't any Healers here. They...they withdrew a long time ago down here. It wasn't anything *I* did, but there haven't been Healers here for at least sixty years."

"There's a Healer here," I said.

"She wouldn't be able to heal him enough to allow him to walk again," Russ said. "It doesn't work like that. Is he strong enough, Ethan?"

"I don't know," Ethan finally said. "He's...he went downhill fast. I don't think he was telling me...us...how bad it was until it was too late."

"What did he say?" Russ asked softly.

"I'm not going to make him into a vampire against his will," Ethan said. "He's asleep now. I don't want to wake him."

"But he spoke to you," I said. "I heard his voice."

"It was the medication talking," Ethan said, and even *I* heard the hopelessness in his voice.

"He said no," Russ whispered.

"Free will," Ethan said. "If I take that away--"

"Maybe you should have living wills for the humans in your family," I suggested. "So you'll know if they're not able to tell you."

"That's a good idea," Ethan said. "Although it doesn't change things now."

"So do what you did with Russ," I said. "Just to get him coherent enough to understand what Russ might be able to do."

Russ shot me a *look;* I ignored him.

"I'm not sure you understand what I *did* to Russ...*for* Russ--" Ethan began.

"I'll call the Healer right now," I said. "It's almost sunset."

"Yes, I *know* that," Ethan snapped.

I pushed back my chair and picked up the landline. Dialed Sennet's number from memory. When she picked up, I said, "Hold on a second, Sennet. Ethan, where *are* you?"

"Paducah," Ethan said.

"Healers go where they are needed, right?" I asked.

"That's right," Sennet said. "Did something happen to Russ?"

"No, he's fine," I said, and Russ shook his head, as if disagreeing with me. "But there's someone in a hospital in Paducah, Kentucky who needs your help. Is there any way you can get to him?"

"Does this have to do with Russ' Kentucky vampires?" Sennet asked.

"Yes," I said.

"Whereabouts in Paducah?" Sennet asked.

I repeated her question to Ethan, who said, "Lourdes Hospital."

"And what, exactly, do they need?" Sennet asked.

"There's a human wizard who is dying," I said. "Ethan needs him strong enough to come here. He's in a wheelchair, usually; he's very weak. Do you think you could go?"

"Ethan needs him strong enough to come here so he can what, make him into a vampire?" Sennet asked.

"So he can ask," I said softly. "And get an answer not muddled by medication."

"I could bring them both here," Sennet said. "But will they have a way to get home? I can't use my portals as a transportation service--"

"Yes," I told her. "We'll drive them back. There's already someone here."

"I can be there in fifteen minutes," Sennet said. "What's Ethan's last name?"

"Walker," I said. "He told us there are no Healers in the vicinity--"

"That doesn't stop me from going," Sennet assured me. "How is Russ, by the way?"

"He's been resting," I said.

"Good," Sennet replied. "Tell Ethan I'll be there shortly."

She hung up the phone; I did the same and glanced at Russ, daring him to say something.

"She's coming," I told Ethan when Russ didn't speak.

"Thank you," Ethan said. "How long will it take her to get here?"

I smiled; I couldn't help it. After meeting Sennet for the first time, I'd realized that Healers were quite adept at their jobs. "About fifteen minutes."

Ethan laughed, then stopped when he realized I wasn't kidding. "You're...serious?"

"Yes," I said. "She'll bring you here, too."

"Oh. I...I don't know what to say," Ethan whispered.

"'Thank you' would work," I said.

"Thank you."

"I'm looking forward to meeting you," I told him, and he said something else, muffled, and then, "She's here."

"Hang up the phone, Ethan," Russ said. "See to Aden. We'll see you soon."

I glanced up to see Niles in the doorway, hanging back, but looking as if he'd been listening for a little while. "Come sit down," I said. "Sennet's there now."

"Who is Sennet?" Niles asked.

"A Healer," Russ said.

"Oh. Then--" He sat down hard in his chair. "Is...is Aden..." His eyes were suspiciously bright.

"They're coming here," I said. "Both of them. With Sennet."

"But Aden--"

"My blood heals vampires," Russ said.

"But Aden was paralyzed as a human," Niles said, not understanding.

"And maybe if he agrees to let Ethan make him into a vampire, my blood could heal him," Russ said. "Maybe. It's worth a try, at least."

Russ didn't look strong enough to try any sort of complicated magic, especially something that had to do with his blood. Niles seemed to think so, too; he started to speak, glanced at me, then shook his head.

"I'm not sure Aden will go for it," he said.

"At least he'll have that choice," Russ said softly.

"I thought he'd *made* his choice," Niles said. "Vampires are, um, they get attached to the humans who live with them. They don't handle it well when we die. *Especially* if they're family."

"Aden's not family," Russ said.

Niles shrugged. "He's not blood kin, but he's family. I think Ethan feels the same about you, too."

"I'm not sure I deserve that, but I'm honored," Russ said.

"Are *you* blood kin?" I asked Niles.

He nodded. "There's a high percentage of humans in the Walker clan."

"I'm not quite sure I know how that works," I admitted, but the phone rang before he could reply.

Russ picked it up first. "Hi, Sennet." He listened. "No, I feel fine. A little tired. I've been resting all day. How's Aden?"

She responded; I couldn't hear what she said. But Russ covered the mouthpiece and said, "He's resting. At Sennet's house. Niles, Karen and I can take you there if you'd like."

"Where's Ethan?" Niles asked.

"With Aden," Russ replied.

"Then I should probably go," Niles said. "If Sennet doesn't mind."

"No, she won't mind," Russ said without asking her. "We'll be there in a few minutes." He hung up the phone. Glanced at me. "Sennet said Aden wouldn't wake up until dawn--"

"So we have time to deliver what Niles found to Sam Rose," I said, and he nodded.

"I want to come with you," Niles said abruptly.

"We'll stop on our way, then," Russ said. He glanced at Niles curiously. "Do you still think they mean us harm?"

"No, I'm just--" Niles flushed. "I don't want anything to happen to you."

"Because of Aden," Russ said.

"Yes."

"I will do my absolute best to stay alive until he makes a decision," Russ promised him, and I saw Niles' eyes widen, as if he hadn't quite expected Russ to go that far.

"Thank you," Niles said.

We packed a few things--some snacks; Russ snagged another bottle of Ethan's restorative. I grabbed my purse and the papers for Sam Rose and we were off, in my car, with the sun only a memory in the sky above us. It was a clear, calm spring evening, only a little nippy. The first stars peeked out of the deep black velvet sky.

It was a quiet evening for traffic. I met no one driving down the road to the detour, of course I shouldn't have met anyone, because of the detour. And the road, still looking lost and forgotten, appeared in my headlights as if it had always been visible; always been there.

"Would I be able to see this if I wasn't with you?" Niles asked.

"I'm not sure," Russ said from where he sat in the back seat. "I really don't know the specifics of this. I've been trying my best not to do magic, just in case that was part of the problem."

Niles turned and stared at him as if he'd grown another head. "You *what?*"

"I guess that doesn't matter now, does it?" Russ asked with false cheer as I turned down the unmarked road.

"I don't know," Niles said, still sounding stunned. "It might."

The end of the road arrived much quicker than I remembered. The cross, the rusting hulk of Sam's car sticking out of the creekbed, the gravel driveway, leading into the forest. There were no ghosts in evidence.

"This is really spooky," Niles said softly. "Did anyone think to bring a flashlight or are we using magic?"

"Magic, I think," Russ said, and the back of the car lit up with a soft silver glow. "Hmm."

As soon as I stepped out of the car, with Russ' light following me, I noticed something different about the setting.

"Didn't you say there was a driveway there before?" Niles asked, and he was right--the gravel drive had vanished, but the cross remained. Neither Sam Rose nor Annabelle appeared.

Russ joined me at the cross. "So what now?" he asked.

"I guess I'll leave the papers here," I said. "And we can come back the next time it rains."

Niles was using a light of his own to inspect the edge of the forest; he stopped at the approximate place the driveway had been and reached out to touch the nearest tree.

"I'd be cautious if I were you," Russ said, and stepped forward as I lay the papers at the foot of the cross. "There's a line that Annabelle cannot cross--"

Something caught his eye, and he reached down to pick up a rock, a piece of gravel from the asphalt. And as Niles turned away from the tree and walked towards him, Russ tossed the stone into the forest.

Nothing reached out to grab them; nothing emerged from the trees. But as Russ turned towards me, I saw his light start to fade. Niles said something, but his voice was drowned out by a rumble of what I thought was thunder, at first, but then realized that it was an engine revving, impossibly loud. Niles and Russ heard it, too; Niles stepped back, into the trees; Russ just stood there, staring, until I pulled him away.

And the car seemed to come out of nowhere, a red sports car, mid-eighties, with a soft top and tinted windows. I turned; as I thought, the car in the creekbed was gone; the oak tree smaller now with less of a spread. It was almost like watching Kyren and Beth; someone's forgotten memory, replayed just for us.

The car passed *through* my car and bounced on the asphalt. Too late, the driver realized that the bridge was out; too late, he slammed on the brakes and tried to stop. He fishtailed; the car ran off the road once, and rolled, landing with a splash in the middle of the creek.

I noticed that the driveway had reappeared. The cross was still there, too, looking worn and faded. Both Russ and Niles seemed just as faded; I'm sure I looked the same to them. *We* were the ghosts here, perhaps.

Niles started to run forward, towards the car, but stopped when neither Russ nor I moved to help the driver.

I caught his arm. "It's not real," I said. "This happened twenty-eight years ago."

"The other car's not there anymore," Niles said, almost frantic. "And you look--"

"We're the ghosts here," I said.

"This has happened to you before," Russ commented, and I nodded, watching the car for any sign of life from the driver.

"With Kyren and Beth. I saw them, in the forest. And the twin Kyren took to Faerie. That's how I found his flute."

"This happens to you often?" Niles asked, his face white.

"*You* live with a vampire," I said, amused.

"But this isn't anything like *that*," Niles said, and wrapped his arms around his stomach. "That...that car just--"

I saw Annabelle first, I think, standing by the oak tree, watching the car with a remote, sad look on her face. She wore different clothes; wilder ones, not the ones she'd worn when she appeared to me and Russ. And she looked different, too; less human, more fae.

But by the time she ended up on the bank of the creek; by the time she reached down to help the eighteen-year-old Sam Rose out of the water--and I hadn't seen any sign of him at all until now; was his body still in the car?--she looked like she had just a day before. Young. Almost glowing as she helped him stand and steadied him on his feet.

Sam asked her a question; she replied, and I wondered if he thought she was an angel, sent to save him from drowning. Was he already dead by then? I thought so.

They walked right past us, Annabelle holding onto his hand, Sam glancing back at the car in the creekbed, a stunned and wondering look on his face. As if he couldn't quite believe what had happened. As if he couldn't quite believe he had survived.

He went with her willingly down the gravel drive, and they disappeared into the darkness, leaving the car behind.

I blinked. The scene faded; the car was now a rusted hulk and nothing more.

"There is just one odd thing," Russ said slowly, as the gravel driveway faded away again.

"Just one?" Niles asked.

"The cross was still there," Russ said, and I realized he was right. "Everything else changed--the trees were smaller; the car; everything. But the cross was still there."

"And that means what?" Niles asked. He looked a bit lost, unused to this even though he *did* live in a vampire's household.

"The cross wasn't put there for Sam," I said. "It was put there for someone else."

"Who?" Russ asked. "Annabelle?"

I turned to face the cross. "No. Not Annabelle. I think...I think we need to go down that driveway."

"What? Now?" Niles asked. "It's not *there*!"

"You looked up the weather for me while you were at the library, didn't you?" I asked. "When is it supposed to rain next?"

"Tomorrow night," Niles said. "Pop-up thundershowers."

Russ looked at me. "What do you want to bet it's raining when we come here tomorrow night?"

"You don't have to come," I said to Niles.

He laughed. "I wouldn't miss it for the world."

I don't back up vehicles well, especially across a long expanse of road. Without the driveway, we couldn't turn around, so with reservations, I let Niles have the wheel. And he managed quite well, for someone who had probably just seen his first ghost.

With Russ giving directions and me in the backseat, we arrived at Sennet's house twenty minutes later. Ethan met us at the door. He wasn't at all what I expected; he looked to be around twenty-five, brown hair, brown eyes, shadowed with grief and something else I couldn't quite place.

"It's okay," Niles said before he could speak.

Ethan nodded. Turned towards me. "You must be Karen."

"Pleased to meet you," I said, and although my first inclination would have been to hug him, I wasn't sure how he'd react, so I settled on a handshake instead.

"I owe you--" Ethan began, but I cut him off.

"No. You're Russ' friend. Any friend of Russ is a friend of mine, and I don't hold debts with my friends." Perhaps my words came out a bit more forceful than I intended; Ethan blinked, staring at me for a moment before offering me a smile.

"Okay," he said. "No debts. But I'll remember this, Karen Montgomery."

I knew it was useless to protest, so I held my tongue. Malachi had tried to explain it to me once, but I still didn't quite understand.

He turned towards Russ, and the smile fell from his lips. "Russ."

"Ethan." Russ sighed. "Stop looking as if I'm carrying a stake behind my back."

"Well, I wouldn't blame you," Ethan said softly, and Niles rolled his eyes. "I should have told you--"

"You should have, yes," Russ said. "But I also didn't ask. I have a couple of questions, though."

Ethan widened his eyes. "Only a couple?"

"About six hundred," Russ said, and smiled. "But a couple will do, for now. How's Aden?"

"Sennet's with him now," Ethan said. "He's still asleep."

"Can I see him?" Niles asked.

"Of course," Ethan said. "He's down the hall. Second door on the right." Niles started down the hall; Ethan stopped him with a question. "Niles, if you were dying, would you want me to make you into a vampire?"

I almost laughed, but laughter would have been completely inappropriate. Still, it was funny to see Ethan take my advice.

Niles turned around. "You'd better," he said.

Ethan nodded. "I'll remember." To Russ, he said, "If you have questions, now would be a good time to ask them."

"Why don't we sit in the kitchen?" I suggested. "I doubt Sennet would mind if we had some tea..." I saw Russ wince. "And I know where she hides the coffee."

Ethan's smile was a fragile thing, and easily broken. "Tea sounds good," he said. "Thank you."

So I made tea, and coffee--Sennet kept hers hidden for guests--and we all sat down at Sennet's kitchen table and Ethan looked more and more uneasy until Russ finally asked, "Will I wake up as a vampire if I die?"

Ethan took a deep breath. "Probably. I'm sorry I don't know for sure. What I...what I did to you has never been done before."

"There's always a first for everything," Russ said lightly. "Karen asked a good question earlier. How long do you plan on keeping me alive?"

"What?" Ethan stared at him, shocked. I think he realized, deep down, that Russ had deliberately changed the wording of my original question, but it was shocking nonetheless. "There wasn't anything else I could do for you," he finally said.

"That's not an answer," Russ replied. "I'd like to know how long I have." He deliberately kept his voice soft. "You've sustained me for three years, Ethan. How much longer before someone refuses to donate?"

"Some of them already have," Ethan said after a moment. "And I haven't insisted."

"The 'free will' thing again," I said.

"Free will is important," Ethan said, and from his tone, I knew I'd offended him. "Especially between vampires and humans. I *could* insist. I could force them. It's not unknown, or even uncommon. But where would that leave me? As it stands, I don't have to be any more on guard than I already am with those of my family and those of my blood."

"They won't betray you because you won't betray them," I said to make up for my previous words, and Ethan nodded.

"Yes."

"Answer my question," Russ said softly. "Please."

"How long would you like to live?" Ethan asked.

"Considering I never expected to make it past my thirtieth birthday, I'm probably already living on borrowed time," Russ replied. "Does it have to be *your* blood? Or is that something else you don't know?"

"It's mostly *my* blood now," Ethan said.

"In that case, how long do *you* intend to live?" Russ asked.

Ethan laughed, but there was no humor in it. "A long time."

"And what happens the day you decide you don't want to--"

I knew what he intended to say and so did Ethan, but Sennet appeared in the doorway before he could finish the sentence. "He's awake," she said simply, and poured herself a cup of tea. "And about as coherent as you're going to get." She shook her head. "And also not very happy with you, Ethan."

Ethan nodded. "I expect he's not."

"What are you going to do if he refuses you?" Sennet asked. "What are you planning?"

"Russ' blood heals vampires," Ethan said softly.

Sennet glanced at Russ. "Heals, like--"

"I don't know," Russ said. "But I'm willing to try it if he's willing to try it."

"And if it doesn't work?" Sennet asked.

"Then at least I'll have given him that chance," Ethan said. "Would you deny him that?"

"I wouldn't deny him anything," Sennet said softly. "But you're forgetting one thing."

"What is that?" I asked.

Sennet spread her hands. "I'm a Healer."

Ethan sat up straight in his chair. "And that means what?"

"He's dying from pneumonia," Sennet said. "Essentially. Brought on by complications of how he got in that chair in the first place. The injury damaged his lungs among other things; I'm surprised he hasn't gotten sick before now."

"You can heal him?" Ethan asked.

"I can't give him the ability to walk again," Sennet said. "I can't heal what is already broken. Maybe if you'd brought him to me right away, and that's just a really big *maybe*. I can, and have, taken care of the pneumonia. But that still leaves him weakened and in a wheelchair. If he stayed here with me, he might recover enough to return to you; otherwise--"

"He could get sick again," Ethan said.

"He *will* get sick again," Sennet replied.

"He wasn't with me when the original injury occurred," Ethan said, and glanced at Russ. It was an involuntary glance; I doubted he intended anything by it, but Russ stiffened anyway.

"No, that was *my* fault," he said. "I did that to him."

Sennet stared at him. "I...imagine you all have quite the interesting history," she said neutrally. "Considering what I know about your background, Russ--"

"Well, he *did* kill my partner first," Russ said. "So what are you saying? He could live as a human and get sick again and maybe die, or you wouldn't have a problem if we try to make him whole again?"

"I'm just saying that you're playing with someone's *life*, here," Sennet said. "It's not just some experiment. It's Aden's entire existence."

"Is he awake and aware enough to make a coherent decision?" Ethan asked.

"He's awake and aware enough to curse you and snarl a bit," Sennet said.

"That sounds like Aden," Ethan said.

Sennet started to speak; I thought she intended to press her point, but Ethan stood up and faced her, and she stared at him for a moment, then nodded.

"I honestly don't believe you mean him any harm," she said.

"Thank you." Ethan hesitated. "My parents were human. My sister is human. I'm not a stranger to loss. I just hate to see someone die before their time."

"And who is the one who decides when someone is dying before their time?" I asked, thinking of Sam Rose.

Sennet stepped out of the doorway. "He's awake," she said. "He won't be awake for long. I'll wait out here."

Ethan nodded and glanced back at Russ, who pushed back his chair and stood.

None of them answered my question, but I didn't really expect them to. "Do you want me to come?" I asked Russ, who nodded.

I followed Russ and Ethan down the hall.

Aden lay in one of Sennet's spare bedrooms--a Healer's house has as many spare bedrooms as the Healer needs at any given time, or so I've been told. He looked to be just a little younger than Russ, but more careworn, if that was possible. Pasty-skinned but bright eyed; I had a feeling that most of his strength came from anger, which he directed at Ethan.

"You can't leave well enough alone, can you?" His voice was raspy and weak.

"Are you feeling better?" Ethan asked, seemingly immune to his anger.

Aden glanced at Russ, then at me, and I saw curiosity struggle to the forefront of his gaze. He tried to glare at Ethan, but he couldn't muster up enough fury. "Yes," he finally said.

"Aden, this is my--" Russ hesitated, glanced at me. "Karen. Karen Montgomery."

"Your Karen," Aden said, and smiled. "Congratulations."

"Thank you," Russ said, and I knew he was close to tears again; his voice cracked. I took his hand.

"It's nice to meet you," I said. "I just wish it were under better circumstances. I've heard a lot about you." That wasn't *entirely* true; I knew the story, of course, but Russ hadn't elaborated. Still, there was something to be said for the fact that when he spoke Aden's name, it was always with warmth. Like the brother he'd never had.

"It's nice to meet you, too," Aden said. "Did they bring you with them to make sure they didn't force me to do anything against my will?" He spoke lightly, but I saw the truth in his gaze; despite Ethan's words, Aden had expected worse of him.

"I wouldn't do that," Ethan protested.

"You would mean well," Aden said. "You always do."

Ethan started to reply, then stopped, but even I could tell that Aden had hurt him. "And now you're baiting him on purpose," I said. "Why? Are you driving away those who care for you because you want to die in peace or because you're afraid you might change your mind?"

Aden stared at me, shocked, his eyes wide. His hands scrabbled over the blankets; he tried to rise, but he couldn't manage to sit up without help even with Sennet's healing. Niles touched his arm; Aden pulled away and then, softly, said, "Please go."

"Aden--" Niles whispered.

"Please go. All of you. Karen can stay." He wouldn't look at anyone else; his gaze was fixed on me.

Russ squeezed my hand, kissed my cheek, and followed Ethan and Niles out the door. They closed it behind them, leaving me alone with Aden, who, finally, closed his eyes and let his head fall back against the pillow.

"I don't want to be a burden for him," he whispered.

"I realize that," I said. "I think he does, too. He just won't admit it. Do you want me to help you sit up?"

"Yes, thank you," Aden said, and I lifted him up and plumped the pillows behind him, adding a few from the pile on the floor until he was comfortably situated.

"Are you thirsty?" There was a pitcher of something on the bedside table, and an empty glass.

"I'm fine," he said. "How long have you known Russ?"

I sat down in Niles' vacated seat. "Seven months."

"You were there when he...almost died," Aden said. "We heard rumors--"

I told him the story, all of it, slightly edited so I wasn't talking for hours. And he listened, his eyes still bright, his breathing steady. And when I was finished, I told him about Naomi and Rosemarie, and everything I *hadn't* told Ethan.

"They seem to think there's a good chance that Russ' blood might heal you if Ethan makes you into a vampire," I said.

"He doesn't owe me this," Aden whispered. His eyes were heavy now; I wondered how much longer he could stay awake.

"I know," I said. "I'm not much on debts, but it seems that you can't escape them."

"I don't want to be a vampire in a wheelchair," Aden said, and roused himself with an effort. He glanced at the pitcher, made an abortive effort to raise his hand, and I poured him some water to drink.

"Do you think it might work?" I asked.

He was silent for a long time. I would have thought he'd fallen asleep, but his eyes were open, glittering in the lamplight.

"Do you know how I came to be with Ethan?" he finally asked.

"No, I don't," I said, and wondered if Russ knew the story.

"The Hunters pretty much murdered everyone in the House I served," Aden said. "I was the only human survivor; there was a vampire, too, but he wasn't in much better shape. Someone heard the commotion and called the police. They took me to a hospital. I was unconscious for three weeks. When I awoke and healed enough to function, they discharged me to a nursing home to learn how to care for myself again."

"That must have been difficult," I said softly.

"It was hell," Aden said. "I had no one; everyone I knew was dead. I had no idea if the Hunters would come back for me; the police were very interested in finding out who had murdered so many people; it was hell. And then, one night, Ethan appeared in my room. He'd heard what had happened, and he'd been looking for me for almost three months. He promised me a place in his House if I wanted it, and anything that would make it comfortable for me to live."

"In exchange for what?" I asked.

"I'm a wizard," Aden said, as if that explained everything. "And he bought me my chair, he made sure most of the house was accessible, he did everything in his power to make sure I felt at home."

"How long have you lived with him?"

"Nine years," Aden said softly. "And he doesn't understand; I'm just getting worse. In nine years, I've progressed from a manual chair to an electric one; my balance is shot, I can't transfer myself anymore, and I've become a burden."

"I don't think he sees you as a burden," I said neutrally.

"I don't see why not," Aden replied. "When I got sick, I just thought...I thought it was time." He looked away, towards the wall, as if embarrassed for me to see his tears.

"And you thought he'd just let you go?" I asked. "Just let you die?"

"He drove me to the hospital himself," Aden whispered. "He carried me to the car. I...I remember that."

"He would do the same for any member of his family," I said firmly, knowing I was right.

"But what if it doesn't work?" Aden asked.

"I don't know," I said. "I wish I did."

Aden nodded and closed his eyes. "Send Ethan in, please," he whispered.

I hesitated, then took his hand. Leaned over, and kissed his cheek. "I think you're very brave."

He laughed, softly. "I'm terrified."

When I opened the door, Ethan straightened up; Russ quirked his eyebrows at me in a silent question. Niles stood with his arms folded, expecting the worst.

"He wants to see Ethan," I said.

"You were in there for almost two hours," Niles said. "And that's all you're going to say?"

"He wants to see Ethan," I repeated. "He doesn't want to be a burden anymore."

"He was never a burden to me," Ethan said, and I was certain he spoke loud enough for Aden to hear.

I just stared at him, perilously on the edge of tears. And he finally understood.

For a moment, he just looked at me. And then, stiffly, he nodded. "Thank you."

He walked past me, and I moved away from the door. But before I closed it, I heard him whisper, "You're very stubborn, you know."

"How could I have survived this long if I wasn't?" Aden replied.

Ethan laughed. "I won't hurt you," he said. "Please don't be afraid."

I pulled the door shut. Turned to face Russ and Niles. "You're going to have to get some rest," I said to Russ.

"Just me?" he asked.

"Maybe Sennet will let us stay here," I said. "Some of us have to go to work in the morning. And later on, they'll need you, I think."

Niles opened his mouth to speak, glanced at the door, and rubbed his eyes. "I think I missed something," he finally said.

"I think you need to rest, too," I replied.

"But I--"

"Two spare bedrooms," Sennet said from the other end of the hall. "That's all I can give you right now."

"We'll manage," I told her. "Thank you."

"But--"

"My blood heals vampires," Russ told Niles, who stared at him in shock, and I realized he hadn't heard that part; hadn't put two and two together until now. "I'm not positive it will work, but I wanted to try, if Aden agreed."

"And if it doesn't work?" Niles managed to ask.

"Then...we'll see," I said, and glanced at Sennet, who nodded.

"Oh...I..." Niles pushed himself away from the wall. He walked over to the door; at first I thought he intended to open it, but he just put his hand against it and then let it fall. And he stared at me, tearblind, until Sennet spoke.

"Niles, why don't you come and sit with me for a little while? I'll make you something to eat."

He seemed happy to have something concrete to hang onto; with one last glance at the door, he walked down the hall to where Sennet waited.

"Fourth door on the left," she said. "Sleep well."

I wasn't sure I'd be able to sleep at all, but I intended to try. I caught Russ' hand and tugged him away from the door. "He'll come for you when it's time," I said, and he followed me down the hall.

This bedroom was almost identical to Aden's room; down to the quilt on the bed.

"We'll have to share," Russ said, suddenly uncertain.

"Get used to it," I said, and he smiled at me.

There were no pajamas; we hadn't packed. But while sleeping in my clothes isn't my most favorite activity in the world, I wanted to be ready just in case something happened.

Neither of us were up to long conversations or anything else, so we climbed into bed and I fell asleep with Russ' arm around me and his breath soft against my cheek.

Sometime during the night, I heard Ethan's whisper from the doorway, and Russ slipped out of bed. He was back before dawn, sprawled next to me with a fresh bandage around his wrist. He didn't wake up when I kissed his cheek, so I left him there and made my way to the kitchen, stopping only to touch the door to Aden's room as I passed.

The smell of perking coffee and frying bacon met my nose as I stepped through the door. Sennet glanced up at my arrival.

"Breakfast?"

"Sounds wonderful," I said. "Have you been up all night?"

She shrugged. "Healers don't need much sleep."

"Still. You don't usually end up with a house full of guests, either," I said, and accepted a cup of coffee.

Sennet poured herself a cup of tea, and waited until I'd filled a plate before joining me at the table with one of her own. She'd scrambled eggs, fried bacon, and even made pancakes, all food that would keep for a while, if needed.

And we ate in companionable silence for a little while, until Sennet said, "Do you have to work today?"

"I should," I said. "If only to make sure the library isn't running itself into the ground."

"Could they spare you for one more day?" Sennet asked, quite seriously.

I glanced at her, wondering if I'd missed something. "I'm sure they could. Is there...something wrong?"

"No, not as such," Sennet said. "It's...a bit more complicated than that."

"Russ?" I asked.

"No. Aden."

"But he...didn't Ethan--"

"I haven't seen Ethan yet," Sennet said. "I only spoke to Russ for a minute before I sent him back to you. I doubt Ethan intended to be this far away from his House right now; otherwise, there wouldn't be any question or issue because there are plenty of humans willing--"

"Oh," I said, inadvertently interrupting her. "To donate."

"Yes. A newborn vampire cannot drink bottled blood. Not for a little while, at least." Sennet smiled, probably at the expression on my face. "If you're not willing, then we'll find someone else. And it's okay. You don't have to. But Niles can't do it all, and I don't think Ethan will ask."

I guess I'd never thought about it. I'd only seen the movies. Even Ivy had been careful to keep that part of her life away from my regard. She'd never asked; I'd never inquired.

"I don't mind," I said, but my voice shook a little; I guess I hadn't ever considered having to do such a thing before.

"I intended to take Ethan in something to drink," Sennet said. "You can come if you'd like."

She prepared another pitcher, but this one wasn't filled with water. A small tray, another cup; I saw a stash of bottles in her pantry, and she smiled when I asked.

"My brother is a vampire."

"I didn't know that," I said.

"His name in Cullen," Sennet said. "He lives in Faerie...not this one... somewhere else. But I like to have something for him to drink when he comes to my house."

"If I'm going to be entertaining vampires in the near future, where would I get bottled blood?" I asked. "Tea works well, under most circumstances--"

Sennet's smile widened. "But tea, alas, cannot sustain the world."

I laughed. "Especially Russ."

"Mmmm, yes," Sennet said. "Now *Russ* is addicted to caffeine." She hesitated. "He told me what happened. If he'd told me that months ago, I never would have suggested he--"

"I know," I said. "And he didn't know. Not for sure." I followed her down the hall.

Sennet handed me the tray and knocked on the door. For a moment, nothing happened. And then the doorknob turned; the door swung open, although Ethan was sitting on the other side of the bed and Aden still lay in the bed, his eyes closed. Sleeping.

Ethan straightened up when Sennet and I walked into the room. He looked...exhausted wasn't quite a strong enough word. He looked bone weary. Hollow-eyed and pale to the point of transparency.

"I brought you something to drink," Sennet said softly, and he nodded, his gaze not on Sennet, but on Aden.

"I have to request one more favor," he whispered. "I hate to ask; I know you said you couldn't take us back, but in any normal circumstance, this wouldn't be an issue."

"Because you'd be home," I said.

Ethan glanced at me. "Yes." He took a drink; some knot of tension visibly faded from the set of his shoulders. "And I have plenty of family to call on there. Here, I only have Niles. And he can't...one human can't--"

"You have me," I said.

"And me," Sennet said. "Although Healer blood is potent, and I can't give him much."

"Will that be enough?" I asked when Ethan didn't answer.

He was staring at us, open-mouthed, his eyes glittering in the lamplight. "Are you *certain*?"

I thought his question was only for me. "Yes. But I do have one question."

"Ask," he said, still stunned.

"Why not Russ?" I thought I knew, but I wanted to hear it from him. Out loud.

Ethan winced. "Russ isn't quite...human anymore. And he's already given Aden blood."

"Alright," I said, surprised I could feel so calm. "What do I need to do? I've never...I've never done this before."

"You don't have to--" Ethan started to say, but Sennet had already extended her wrist to Ethan, calm, serene. I wondered if she'd ever lost her temper.

And Ethan, with a glance at me, raised her wrist to his lips and *bit*. And then, careful not to waste a drop, he guided Sennet's wrist to Aden's mouth.

"It will heal without a scar if I...if you don't use a knife," he said, and I heard the embarrassment in his voice.

"That's good to know," I said softly.

His smile flew across his lips. "I tried to convince Russ of that, but he didn't want--" His voice trailed away.

"Ethan, it's okay," I said. "I trust you."

"I'm glad," he whispered. "Because I have no choice but to trust *you*."

It only seemed a few minutes later when Sennet stepped away and it was my turn. My hand shook when I held it out to Ethan, but he did not mention it; he gently took my hand and raised it to his lips. "I won't hurt you," he whispered, and bit deep.

And...it *didn't* hurt. It throbbed, but not with pain; with another, different feeling that I wasn't sure how to define. Ethan raised his head from my wrist.

"*You* aren't completely human, either," he said, holding his thumb over the wound he had made.

I had forgotten. The fact that Kyren was my great-great grandfather seemed so commonplace nowadays that I hardly even thought of it anymore. "I'm sorry. My mother's grandfather was an elf. *Is* an elf. His name is Kyren. We've met. Is that a problem?"

I knew I was babbling, but I couldn't seem to shut up.

Ethan grew very still, staring at me. "You have elvish blood?"

"Very diluted," I said.

"Does that make a difference?" Sennet asked from behind me.

"Elvish blood doesn't dilute well," Ethan said, and for a moment, I thought he would send me out of the room. "It's intoxicating. And powerful. Even diluted." He smiled. "Yet another reason why elves don't care for vampires."

"Will my blood hurt Aden?" I asked.

"No. It won't hurt him. It will probably help him just as much as Sennet's blood." Ethan guided me over to the bed, his thumb still pressed across my wrist. "Just...I wouldn't advertise the fact that you have elvish blood to too many vampires."

"I won't," I promised him, and he gently pressed my wrist over Aden's mouth. And if he licked his thumb as he turned away, I did not care, because

Aden's eyes flickered open, and his hand rose to grasp my wrist--lightly--and he drank.

Sometime later, Russ kissed my cheek. "Karen?"

I opened my eyes, confused at first, because I wasn't sitting on the edge of Aden's bed anymore; I was lying down. On Sennet's couch, with a pillow under my head and a blanket draped across me. My mouth was terribly parched, my lips dry.

The first thing Russ gave me when I sat up was a glass of water, the second, a cup of coffee.

"Bless you," I said, and took a grateful sip. "What happened?"

"You'd never donated blood to a vampire before," Russ said. "It can be a little overwhelming."

"To what, my head?" I asked, and rubbed my temples. "I don't feel bad or anything, just a little tired." I sat up straight. "Oh, crap! I didn't call in to work!"

"Already taken care of," Russ said, and sat beside me. "But your director said if she doesn't hear from you by tomorrow morning, she's going to hunt me down to make sure you're okay. I told her you'd call."

I laughed. "I'll call. How's Aden?"

"Talking," Russ said. "Sitting up." Something passed across his face, then, and I realized what hadn't happened.

"It could take some time," I told him.

"I know," Russ said.

"How is he otherwise?" I asked.

"Definitely Aden," Russ replied. "Do you want to sit with him for a little while? I'm sure Niles could use a break, and Ethan will probably sleep for the rest of the afternoon."

"How do *you* feel?" I asked.

"I'm fine," Russ said. "I slept longer than you did, after all. And I've done this before. Many times."

I stared at him for a long moment, just *looked* at him until I could convince myself that he wasn't leaving anything out. "Good. Where's Sennet?"

"Out," Russ said. "On a call. She said we were on our own for lunch, so I picked something up when I went to get your bag and a change of clothes."

"A change of clothes sounds fabulous," I said. "And I'd be happy to sit with Aden for a while. What are *you* going to do?"

"Sit with you," Russ said promptly. "There's only one chair, but I'm sure I can snatch one from somewhere else."

"That sounds good to me," I said, and drained the rest of my coffee. "Where's my bag?"

Thirty minutes later, I'd made my call to the director, assured her that I wasn't being held hostage, *and* I'd changed my clothes, brushed my teeth, eaten a fast food sandwich for lunch, and had another cup of Russ' coffee. Russ liberated a chair from Sennet's kitchen, I settled into the comfy chair beside Aden's bed, and we sent Niles off to rest.

Aden was asleep, curled on his side, his hair half-covering his face, the shadows under his eyes gone now, the waxy sheen of his skin no longer quite as evident.

It was nice to be with someone who didn't *have* to have conversation to fill in the silence. It was nice to lean against Russ as well, and hold his hand.

Russ traced the ring on my finger. "So have you had a chance to think about the house?"

"The house is wonderful," I said. "I would love to live there, as long as Peter doesn't mind a bit of redecorating."

Russ smiled. "I don't think he'll mind unless you want to get rid of a few books."

"I would never do that," I said automatically.

"I know." Russ hesitated. "You don't have a problem with...me? I'm not going to be able to stop drinking Ethan's potion. If he decides to stop making it--"

"He won't," Aden said from the bed. "He feels responsible for what happened to your family, even though he's not." He rolled over awkwardly and I moved to help him, but he waved me away. "I can manage, but thank you."

And he *did* manage, quite adeptly. Although in the end, I had to help him with the pillows.

"And, god forbid, but what if Ethan dies?" Russ asked. "I'm not sure I want that hanging over our heads for--"

I kissed him, just to shut him up. "It doesn't matter," I said. "Well, it matters, but not in the way you think it does. I'm not going anywhere, no matter what happens."

I saw Aden smile. Russ stared at me for a moment, then shook his head.

"I don't deserve you."

Aden laughed.

"Maybe not, but you've got me," I said. "Although I really think we're going to have to do something about that van of yours."

Russ backed away from me in mock horror. "The van runs fine!"

I turned towards Aden. "How do you feel?"

"Better," he said, still smiling at our antics. "Every time I wake up I feel stronger."

"Still no--" Russ began.

"I have a theory about that," Aden said.

"After less than a day as a vampire?" Russ asked.

"Well, it takes time for muscles to heal, doesn't it?" Aden asked. "So it would make sense if it didn't happen right away...if it's going to happen at all. I guess we'll have to wait and see."

"Can you feel *anything*?" I asked.

Aden shot me a look that was half frightened, half hopeful, but wholly human. "Well."

"'Well' sounds promising," Russ said slowly.

Aden struggled with the covers for a moment, and I helped him push them away. He wore a hospital gown with a t-shirt over top of it, and his legs were pale and white and wasted. "I guess I'm going to need some clothes," he said softly. "And I don't think Ethan had a chance to bring my chair."

"You can borrow some of my clothes," Russ said.

"Thank you." Aden ran one hand through his hair and made it stick up in clumps. "And a shower would be nice."

"I'm sure that can be arranged," I promised him. "We'll even help you out to the kitchen if you don't want to stay in here--"

"Watch," Aden said. "Look at my feet."

We obeyed. Aden whispered something under his breath; it sounded like a prayer. I felt no sign of magic, just his concentration, focused on his feet. And, very faintly, barely a quiver--his toes *twitched*. All of them. At once.

"It comes and goes," he said, and I dared not look at his face for fear I would glimpse his tears. "But that has to be a good sign, don't you think?"

"May I?" Russ asked, and reached down.

"Go ahead," Aden whispered.

Russ touched the arch of Aden's foot and gently, softly, drew his finger down the pale white skin; barely touching.

Aden's foot *jerked*. Spasmed, perhaps. He fell back against the pillows. "I...I *felt* that. Don't do it again. It hurt."

"I'd say that's a good sign, then," Russ said softly. "I'm sorry I hurt you."

I met Aden's gaze. His eyes were swimming in tears. "You didn't think it would work," I said. "Did you?"

He shook his head. "No."

"It still might take a while for mobility," Russ said. "For you to gain control. But you have time."

"Yes," Aden said, quiet now. "I have time."

Between us, Russ and I managed to help him up, and to the bathroom--he chased us out, then, insisting that he knew what he was doing and had no intention of drowning. Russ gathered him up some clothes; they were too big on Aden, of course, but they were clothes and not a hospital gown.

By the time Ethan awoke a few hours later, Aden was sitting at the kitchen table, clean and dressed, drinking tea for his lunch--or supper, by then--while Russ and I made dinner for the humans and Niles sat and watched. Sennet had not returned, but she had called for an update.

Ethan stopped in the doorway. Niles slid back his chair and stood up. "You can sit here," he said before anyone could offer him a seat.

"I can stand just as well," Ethan said, and although he still looked tired, he managed to favor Niles with a smile. "But thank you."

"There's bottled blood in the pitcher," I said. "Can Aden drink it now or will he need more of ours?"

"I wasn't sure," Aden said when Ethan didn't immediately reply.

"You can drink it now, I think," Ethan said. To me, he said, "You don't want to donate so soon again. Believe me when I say that." He glanced at Aden. "You look much better."

Aden smiled, briefly. "I moved my toes. On one foot."

"We'll have to work getting your muscles back in working order," Ethan said, and when Niles made no move to sit down, he sighed and took his seat. "I believe the humans call it physical therapy. I took the liberty of visiting that section of the hospital while we were there--"

Aden's eyes narrowed. "I've been through physical therapy. It was torture."

"As a human," Ethan said. "Not as a vampire."

"True," Aden said, considering. "I'm willing to try." And then his mind caught up with Ethan's words. "You...you *knew* I would--"

"I *hoped*," Ethan said, and I saw a bit of how he managed his household now; in his bearing and his gaze. "I like to plan for the future." He smiled. "If it helps, I also made sure there was room for you in the family vault."

"But I'm not a Walker," Aden said.

Ethan shrugged. "You might as well be. And you don't have any other kin."

Aden couldn't reply to that.

"It's almost sunset," Russ said. "You're welcome to bunk in my house for a little while, and Karen has a spare bedroom, too. We probably should give Sennet her house back. If you want to stay for a little while."

"You said I could go with you tonight," Niles said to me, and for a moment, I had no idea what he was talking about.

"Oh, right," I said. "Is it raining yet?"

Both Ethan and Aden looked mystified. As I served up supper--just a tuna casserole, nothing more--Russ told them about Annabelle and Sam Rose.

"This has to do with your Council?" Ethan asked when he was finished. I wondered how much he knew about the Council.

"No, not yet," Russ said. "Just curiosity, so far. If we have to call the Council, it would have to be for something more than a ghost."

"Annabelle sounds like she's a bit more than a ghost," Ethan said. "They don't mind if you poke around like this?"

I smiled. "Why would they mind? We're doing their work for them."

"In a way," Russ said, and I shrugged.

"In the original definition of the Council, we are," I said. "In the modern definition, there aren't enough members to go around."

"Maybe you should join," Aden said, and I thought he was joking at first.

"I'm not a wizard," I told him. "I can't see where I'd bring much to the group."

"You're not completely human," Ethan pointed out. "And you evidently can see ghosts; there has to be *something* there--"

I didn't want to get in a long conversation about my lack of magical talent. "I'm very happy with being a librarian," I said. "And anyway, I'm not the one who got an invitation to join."

Ethan glanced at Russ. *"You?"*

"I haven't accepted yet," Russ said mildly.

"But you will," Aden said.

Russ hesitated, then nodded. "Probably. They need help. There are only two Council members, Lucas and Niklas, and--"

"Wait one second," Niles said, balancing his plate in one hand as he forked food into his mouth. "There are only two Council members? *The Council?* The same ones everyone is afraid of?"

"Well, they do have the Hunt on their side," I said. "That has to count for something."

"Well, if it's not true what they say about the Council, then is it true what they say about the Hunt?" Aden asked.

"What do they say about the Hunt?" Russ replied, then smiled when no one answered. "I'm sure the Hunt knows what 'they' say about them."

"I take it you're good friends with them as well," Ethan said. "I...I heard they had something to do with Andre's death."

"They had *nothing* to do with Andre's death," I said, a trifle sharper than I intended. "Andre *fell* to his death. That much is true."

"The fact that there was a very large dragon behind him and a Hound before him has nothing to do with it," Russ said, straight-faced.

"I think Josiah would take issue with that," I said.

"And Josiah is--" Ethan began.

"A Hound," I said. "The youngest Hound, and also the Hunt's wizard."

"*And* you're on first-name basis with the Wild Hunt?" Aden asked. "The Council would be stupid if they didn't ask you to join."

I smiled at him. "I can arrange an introduction if you'd like. I'm sure the Hunt would love to meet you."

Niles choked on a mouthful of tea. Aden twisted around and grabbed Niles' plate before it could fall. He'd moved sideways in his seat; I don't think he realized he was bracing himself with one leg--his foot automatically outstretched--until the muscles in his leg started to shake and he started to slide.

Ethan caught him, Russ rescued the plate, and Sennet stepped into the kitchen behind Niles and touched his arm.

He drew in a breath. Coughed. Carefully set the mug down on the table. Realized all eyes were upon him and flushed. "I'm fine."

Aden straightened up in his seat, gave Ethan an almost frightened glance, and then, with an audible shake in his voice, said, "That hurt."

"Physical therapy," Ethan said.

"Why don't we see what you can do so far?" Sennet asked, and Aden nodded, his gaze still on Ethan.

"Come on," Ethan finally said. "You can lean on me. We'll go into the living room--if Sennet doesn't mind."

"And we should be going, too," Russ said. "Ethan, you don't mind if Niles comes with us?"

"I don't mind," Ethan said. "Just please don't get him killed."

"I'll do my best," Russ promised, and I don't think he was joking at all.

It was raining by the time we got to the main road; a soft, steady rain that pattered against the windshield and ran in rivulets down the glass. Russ had opted for the back seat; Niles sat beside me on the edge of his seat, straining to see farther than the headlights in the darkness.

He didn't really have to strain. As soon as I spotted the cross, Sam Rose appeared in front of my car, standing in the rain as if he'd been waiting for an eternity. He held the sheaf of papers in one hand.

I stopped the car. We all got out, standing a little awkwardly in front of him, blinking in the rain.

"Come with me," he said.

"Where?" Russ asked.

Sam gave him a *look*. "I think you know."

"And we're just supposed to *trust* you?" Niles asked.

Sam *looked* at him, too, but Niles wasn't fazed. "You would rather stand out in the rain?" he finally asked. "It's not raining past the driveway."

I touched Niles' arm. "It's okay."

"How do you *know*?" he asked, and I had to remind myself that he lived with a vampire, and all the natural paranoia that seemed to come with that.

"I don't," I said. "But it's okay. This seems awfully elaborate if the point was to get us down that driveway in the first place. I think something else is going on."

"I agree," Russ said, and followed Sam Rose across the road, over the line that Annabelle could not cross, and onto the gravel driveway. "Huh. It's *not* raining here."

Niles and I followed, slower, because there was something different again, about the scene. The cross was still there; the car still sat in the middle of the creek, but the oak tree--

Had split. I hadn't noticed it because it looked fine on the other side. But once we passed the invisible line; once Niles and I stepped onto the gravel, the oak tree practically withered and died in front of my eyes.

"So where *are* we?" Niles asked.

"Not in Faerie," Russ said. "Not quite in the human world, either."

"We are *between*," Sam Rose replied. He indicated the oak tree. "It is still alive on your side."

"What does that mean?" I asked.

"It means what it means," Annabelle said from a few feet away.

Niles jumped. I grabbed his arm.

"You brought papers," Annabelle continued, her voice soft. "You told him what happened afterwards."

"We looked it up in the newspaper archives at the library," I said. "Well, Niles did."

"There was no afterwards for me," Annabelle said. She looked lost now, a child, nothing more. Maybe twelve, thirteen; her eyes wide under her too-big hat.

"Was the cross put here for you?" Russ asked gently.

Annabelle smiled, a trifle sadly. "No, not me. The oak is--was--my monument, as Sam's car is his."

"What lies at the end of this driveway?" Niles asked, and Annabelle favored him with a sunny smile.

"That is what you came here to find out," she said.

"Do *you* know?" Sam Rose asked.

Annabelle hesitated. Glanced at him. "No. No, I don't. I can't...I can't go past a certain point. I've seen the house, but I haven't approached it."

"You told me--" Sam began.

"To pass the time," Annabelle whispered. "To share a story. I didn't want you to go away." She twisted her hands together, staring at him; at us. "I'm sorry."

"The house?" I asked.

Annabelle shifted from one foot to the other. "There is a house at the end of the driveway," she said.

"I didn't know that," Sam said. "What *else* haven't you told me?"

"That I don't know why we are trapped here," Annabelle said. Her voice was very small. "I am glad you had an afterwards."

Sam glanced at us, obviously regretting the audience. And I wondered if Annabelle would have been so forthcoming without us there; we were on *her* territory now, or between. Whatever that truly meant.

"The house, then?" I asked, and Russ nodded. "How far away is it? Can we drive, or are we walking?"

I turned around; my car still sat on the road, unmolested.

"We'll walk," Russ said with a funny little hitch in his voice. I turned around to face him.

We hadn't moved, but the driveway had shortened. Now, instead of a long length of gravel, we stood on asphalt, and a cute little white bungalow stood less than fifty yards away, its windows blank; the flowerbeds neglected.

Russ looked as if he'd seen a ghost--or something terrible, but it only looked like a house to me. Niles was staring at Russ with shock and fear and pity in his gaze.

I caught Russ' arm as he stepped past me. "Wait a minute."

When he turned to look at me, I swear he saw something else. "Russ. Wait a minute." I glanced at Annabelle. "What do *you* see when you look at that house?"

"It is not the same house I saw before," Annabelle said, and I saw only puzzlement in her gaze. "The other house was larger. Brick."

Russ closed his eyes.

"Whose house is this?" I asked softly.

"His," Niles whispered. "The house where--"

"Naomi and Rosemarie died," Russ finished, his voice low, toneless.

"You came for him," I said to Niles, who nodded. "Russ, that's not your house."

"I realize that," Russ said, and managed to give me a little smile. "But...what will we find *inside*?"

Meaning, would we walk inside to find his family dead again? Was this some sort of protective spell? Or worse?

"We're not going inside," I said.

"I think we have to," Russ said, still facing me, facing the way back to my car as well. I looked; I had to, even though I saw the truth in his gaze.

The road behind us was gone, and so were Annabelle and Sam. Behind us, only forest, thick and dim and dark. In front, the white house beckoned, and an early tulip bobbed in the sudden breeze.

"I'd die happy if I never saw another ghost," Niles said. "I think I'll stick with vampires."

Russ laughed.

"Can you ward yourself against this?" I asked. "Against whatever is using your memories?"

Russ murmured something under his breath, then shook his head when the house remained as it was. "I feel *something*," he said, and glanced at Niles for corroboration. "But I think we need to see this through first." He hesitated, though, unwilling to take the first step. And Niles seemed to be similarly petrified.

"What did you see when you walked through the door?" I asked.

"Candles," Russ said. "All over the living room. He lit candles. Everywhere."

I walked up the short path to the front door, leaving them behind. When I opened the door, I half-expected to *see* candles everywhere, but the room was empty, hollow, cold.

"It's empty," I reported, and Russ closed his eyes again. A moment later, he joined me on the stoop and glanced inside. And some of the terrible tension drained out of his bearing. I took his hand and glanced at Niles, who was right behind us. "It's empty."

"Thank goodness," Niles said fervently.

I flipped the light switch. Weak yellow light illuminated the rest of the living room and chased away most of the shadows. It was still empty.

Slowly, together, we stepped inside.

The kitchen and the living room/dining room were connected by a little bar area, the appliances and cabinets were still in place but they looked old and unused. Dusty, too. Motes of it danced and sparkled in the air around us. I wondered if the dust itself was cause for concern.

We moved from the living room down a hallway; Russ led now, I was in the middle and still holding his hand. He seemed to know which door to open, and he stood there for a moment with his hand on the doorknob, his head bent, his eyes closed.

"Are you sure you want to do this?" Niles asked.

"It's a memory of the house and nothing more," Russ whispered, but he sounded like he was trying to convince himself of that. Before he could hesitate any longer, he pushed open the door.

This room was simply furnished, with a bed, a nightstand, a dresser, a chair. The shadowy figures lying on the bed--dim in the darkness--were, of course, Naomi and Rosemarie, but Russ seemed to expect that.

"There was a lamp before," he said, almost harshly. "A lamp. I didn't turn on the overhead light because I was afraid Andre had rigged it or something. I walked across the room like this--" He walked across the room, angry now. "And I reached for the lamp--" He reached for the lamp which wasn't there, and the figures on the bed subtly faded. "And I turned it on. And I saw my murdered family--my wife and my baby daughter--and *why don't you get out of my memories?*"

When he turned towards us, there was spellfire in the palm of his hand. It flickered off his features and made him look positively demonic.

"I wanted to burn down the house," he said in a calmer voice. "I wanted to join my family, but I didn't. Ethan--and Niles and Dahlia--came and stopped me."

"Well, then, burn it down," Niles said. "Burn it down now, only not with us inside, if you please."

Russ stared at him for a moment. I gaped at him.

But then, Russ said, "Yes."

The figures on the bed were almost gone now; I could see the wall through the bed itself. The nightstand had disappeared; the chair--well, I wouldn't have sat in the chair for any amount of money.

Russ walked over to us. "Let's go," he said. "I can set a spell inside to go off when we leave, and we'll be done with this."

"That won't help Sam and Annabelle," I said, and he gave me a *look* which made me realize that I'd missed something.

And then I realized what it was. "Maybe it will," I told him. "If you burn down this house and it's the cause--"

"Please don't," a small voice whispered.

"Tell me why I shouldn't," Russ countered, still angry.

"Because this is my home," the voice said, and the walls around us faded away, shifted, morphed, until we stood inside a cabin, not a house. One room; a dirt floor. The roof had vanished long ago; the walls were intact, great severed trunks of trees that no longer grew in these forests.

Niles whispered something under his breath that sounded like a curse.

The voice belonged to a little girl, or, I saw a moment later, a small person, dainty and tiny, hardly taller than a four-year-old human. She stood beside a seedling tree that had sprouted in the corner of the cabin--an oak, I realized. Like the walls around us.

Only log cabins weren't usually made of oak. I mean, it had been known to happen, but that wasn't a normal type of wood to use.

The thicknesses of the trunks used in for the cabin's walls made me think of Riyanna's mother, and her grove in Faerie. Had there been an earlier grove here that someone had cut down?

"*You* are not the cause of this," Russ said after a moment, and the little girl shook her head.

"It is the wizard," she said, and motioned to the opposite wall. "His hatred still lingers."

"The wizard?" Niles asked.

As soon as he spoke, I saw it--a skeleton, human in shape, at least; I'd mistaken the bones for branches, bleached by wind and rain. He lay on what used to be a bed in the corner, rotten now, but still with the remnants of carvings on the one remaining post.

Most of the corner was covered by acorns; a great wash of them, brittle and cracked, dead and decayed. What wasn't covered by acorns had been buried by leaves; the skull crushed by a log, perhaps from the roof or the trees overhead.

"Who was the wizard?" I asked.

The girl shrugged. "He was here when I rooted," she said, cementing her identity in my mind. "And I felt his hatred. My kin--" Here, she touched the nearest wall gently. "My kin died for him, and not willingly. He knew what he attempted, and he failed."

"Your kin," Russ said slowly, and reached out to touch the closest wall.

"Yes. Ancient kin, but kin indeed."

I glanced at Niles to see how he was taking this; his gaze was on the skeleton and the pile of acorns and leaves. "Did they get their revenge?" he asked, his voice soft.

"They got their justice," the girl replied. "I would not count sacrificing children as revenge."

Children? I almost asked, but then I realized what she meant. The acorns. I reached down to pick one up; it was surprisingly heavy, despite its age. "You just--cast your seeds to the wind and hope they take root?"

"Once, we had groves," the girl said. "Where the children could grow in peace with plenty of sunlight."

"There is one such grove in Faerie," I said. "I'm sure you would be welcome there."

"But I have already rooted," the girl said.

"We couldn't...we couldn't just dig you up?" Niles asked hesitantly.

The girl stepped back, her face suddenly full of fear, as if she expected us to tear her spindly little tree out by its roots.

"That's not how it works," Russ said. "Right? Where you root is where you stay? Even if it's not a good location?"

"Yes," the girl said, her voice soft. She glanced at Niles; he seemed a bit lost.

"The way Riyanna's mother explained it, the grove feeds the oaks who live there," I said. "There is a mother tree; there are never too many children. Not all of the acorns are fertile."

"You know a dryad, too?" Niles asked, almost disbelieving.

"It's a long story," I said. "Before I met Russ."

"So what would *you* need to flourish?" Russ asked. "And none of this explains Annabelle or Sam Rose. Or the cross."

The girl clearly had no idea what we were talking about.

"There are two ghosts trapped at the end of the driveway," I said. "One is...well, she might be the spirit of an oak tree. The other is a human man, although he was a boy when he died. And there's a cross that marks the spot for someone else--it's too new to be for your wizard, though."

"The cross must be for the other one," the girl said.

"The other one?" Niles repeated, and she pointed again, out into the forest behind the cabin.

"My kin tell me he tried to break the wizard's hold on this place, and failed. That is when they sacrificed the children." She paused, listening to something we couldn't hear. "There was a girl. She got away."

"Annabelle?" I asked aloud. But that made no sense. Annabelle was tied to the oak tree, just as this girl was tied to hers. Trapped, yes, but still tied.

"Why don't we ask the 'other one', if we can find him?" Russ asked.

"This is *his* between," the girl whispered. "I do not know if he will speak to you."

"You never answered my question," Russ said gently. "What would you need to flourish?"

The girl's smile was fleeting and quick as she stepped back against her tree. "I cannot flourish here. Not like this." She touched the wall again, a tiny caress. "But others could, if you give them a place to grow."

"But--you'll *die* without a good place to grow," Niles said.

"It is where I've rooted," the girl replied, her voice soft. Accepting of her fate.

"And if we could guarantee to keep all of your roots intact?" Russ asked. "And we promised to plant your tree in a bright sunny spot where you could have a grove of your own?"

The girl was already shaking her head. "What you propose is impossible," she said. "You could not protect *all* of my roots."

Russ looked as if he wanted to pursue this; as if he wanted to show her that he could do such a thing, but I knew the girl would never agree to it. Dryads were funny that way. Just the fact that Riyanna existed was an anomaly; they never would have considered such a thing before now.

"Where will we find the 'other'?" I asked.

"Behind the cabin," the girl said.

"And what did the wizard do to him?" Niles asked.

The girl touched the wall again, and listened to the voice, or voices, we could not hear. "They say he is entombed," she said. "And he dreams."

"He's *alive*?" I asked.

The girl hesitated. "He is not...alive. Not in the way you mean. But he *was* a wizard."

"And wizards do not die like other men," Russ muttered under his breath, and I wondered if he was quoting someone. It sounded like something Lucas would say.

We left the girl and the wizard's skeleton then, and walked outside into thick forest. The undergrowth almost buried the cabin from the outside;

there were vines *everywhere;* vines and rosebushes that were in too much shade to bloom.

Behind the cabin, there was a pile of rubble, or what *looked* like a pile of rubble, at least at first. It had been an icehouse, perhaps, a small, stone building carved out of a hillside, the door gone; half one wall obliterated by the roots of the tree that had sprouted atop it.

The tree was not an oak. It was a twisted, ugly thing with thorns six inches long, bristling from every branch. Its leaves, barely peeking out of tightly curled buds, were tipped with red.

The girl hadn't told us, but we moved towards the building anyway; it was the only obvious choice for someone to be entombed within. Russ lifted a curtain of vines that hung across the doorway; Niles called up a light, and we all peeked inside.

The tree's roots had spread across every surface; invaded every orifice of the little building and the young man who lay within. His skin was covered with them, reaching into his eyes, his nose, his mouth; spread across his skin like faint, pale tattoos. And yet, he breathed under his curtain of roots.

Or the tree breathed for him. Even as Niles' light lit up the room, a thin shaft of sunlight fell across the young man's outstretched leg and the roots that covered his skin in that one specific spot crumbled to ash in an instant. The young man's body jerked; he twisted sideways, or tried to, but he was held fast by the roots.

"Vampire," Russ breathed, and threw up a ward that blocked the sunlight. "She could have told us he was a *vampire.*"

"I doubt she knows," I said. "Is he--*alive?*"

"How long can a vampire live without eating?" Niles asked.

"Live?" Russ barked a laugh. "They can *live* for a very long time. Don't ask me how I know. They can live, but they can't *exist;* they lose themselves.

Their identity. Their minds." He studied the vampire; the roots, the tree above. "This isn't...there's something wrong. The tree is feeding--"

"Off a vampire," I said, sickened.

"The roots only lead to him," Russ whispered.

"If we cut down the tree, will he die?" Niles asked.

Russ ran one hand through his hair. "I don't know. It might be best if he did. There might not be much to save."

The vampire had not moved again. His eyes remained closed, covered by roots finer than a strand of hair.

"Well, now would be your chance to prove to the little oak tree back there that you really *could* move her safely," I said, and motioned towards the network of roots. "If you could free *him,* then she should be a piece of cake."

"But what would I be setting free?" Russ asked. "We only have the dryad's word, her 'ancient kin' that this isn't the wizard. What if the skeleton in the cabin belongs to the 'other'?"

"And this is the wizard?" I asked doubtfully.

"I would feel much better about this if I had my computer," Russ muttered.

"Oh!" Niles dug into his pocket and tossed Russ a small handheld. "Will this help?"

Russ smiled. "Absolutely," he said, and turned it on.

I'm still not sure how Russ makes the computers do magic, but I'm fairly certain you can't buy that kind of software in the stores. At least not the kind that really works. He made it scan the vampire's body; an image of the roots showed up on the tiny screen, a puzzle too intricate to solve.

"Hmm."

"That doesn't sound promising," Niles said, and Russ showed him the screen, and they conversed in low voices about technical this-and-that, and I tuned them out because I had no idea what they were talking about.

I walked along the wall instead, touching the roots that protruded from the stone, watching the vampire for any sign that he felt my touch...to no avail. I almost missed the backpack tucked into a corner; the leather blended in with the tree roots that had curled around it.

There was a bottle, too, broken; entwined in roots. I wondered if it had once contained blood.

The backpack resisted my efforts to unearth it; the roots were thick here. I broke one and a small rivulet of soil sprinkled down on my head as if the tree itself had protested.

The vampire made a noise, a cross between a protest and a whimper.

"What are you doing?" Russ asked, noticing I was gone for the first time.

I freed the backpack without breaking any other roots and opened the top flap.

"Dennis Joseph Sawyer," I said when I found the vampire's wallet with an actual license within. I held it up for Russ' inspection. "The license expired in 1958." There was a folded piece of paper, brittle with age, inside the backpack as well, with the name 'Josephine' written on the outside. And other, mundane items, including an unopened bottle, probably blood. A pocketknife, its blade blackened. A book--I thought it was blank, at first, but when I opened it, I realized it was a journal.

"A spell journal," Russ said when I showed it to him. "This address is in Iowa; what was he doing out *here?*" He unfolded the piece of paper, and holding it carefully, began to read.

"'My darling Josephine,

If you find this, then I am gone. Take Matthieu and the baby to my family's home in Maine and give them the pendant I gave you when we were wed. They will take care of you and keep you safe.

I am sorry that I failed you. I hope this finds you well.

All my love,
Joseph."'

I had to blink away the tears in my eyes before I could speak. "Did she get away?"

"If Annabelle is Josephine, then no, I don't think so," Russ said, staring at the vampire's body. "If she's not; if she's just caught in this like Sam is--"

"Then maybe Josephine escaped," Niles said. "The dryad said there was a girl--"

"But what were they doing *here?*" Russ asked.

"We need more information," I said. "Does that computer of yours have a phone?"

"There's no service out here," Russ said absently. "And--"

"What is he holding in his hand?" Niles asked, and for the first time I saw that the vampire's right hand, *Joseph's* hand, was tightly clenched. And oddly free of roots.

Before Russ could stop me, I knelt down and gently eased his fingers apart. They were freezing cold, and resistant to my efforts, but I managed to uncover a glass ball, slightly larger than a marble, that started to glow as soon as I touched it.

The vampire's body went rigid. I heard a gasp; heard him choking, no doubt on the roots, and then Russ, above me, muttering under his breath, holding the handheld above me like a portable x-ray machine.

"Hold his hand," he snapped when I started to move away; I did as he asked and he continued to mutter. Niles' voice soon joined him. And the vampire's hand clenched over mine; he was trying to breathe now; but I knew the roots had grown into his lungs; he was gasping, struggling, still unable to move.

Russ whispered something that sounded like a prayer. "Is it day or night outside?"

"It was night when we started, but the sun--" Niles began.

I glanced outside. "Dusk."

"When I tell you to grab him, grab him and pull him outside," Russ said. "Don't hesitate; I think the roof will come down when I sever the connection. Pull him outside--"

"What about you?" Niles asked, his eyes wide.

"I'll be right behind you," Russ said.

"But--"

"Don't hesitate," Russ said. "Go. *Now.*"

He spoke one word; just one, and flung out his hand. Fire arced from his fingers, not burning, but slicing through the roots with laser-like precision. Niles and I grabbed Joseph's arms and legs and pulled him out across the ground as the walls quaked around us; we didn't have time to stop and watch the tree fall or the walls crumble.

I *thought* Russ was right behind us. I *thought* I felt his hand on my arm, for a moment, at least. I know I saw the marble fall from Joseph's hand and roll into the icehouse, still glowing brightly. I know I saw the vampire open his eyes.

And then something *rolled* through the ground; not an earthquake, but an explosion. I fell; I couldn't help it, the ground was no longer beneath my feet. The explosion rippled out across the forest, and something--some invisible curtain--*tore* in two.

Someone grabbed my arm. Hauled me backwards. I saw the far wall of the cabin collapse in slow motion, outward, not inward. But I'd been facing the stone building, not the cabin. I started to turn around.

"Steady now," Sam Rose said from beside me.

I stared at him, momentarily speechless.

"You hit your head when you fell," he said. "How do you feel?"

Panic was slow to push past shock. "Russ!"

He tried to stop me, but I tore out of his grasp. "Karen, wait--"

I skidded to a stop six feet away from what had once been an icehouse and a vampire's tomb, but now was a pile of rubble and branches, nothing more.

"Russ!" I shouted his name, willing him to answer.

A few of the trees surrounding the building were leaning drunkenly; one had split in two. Niles lay on the ground behind me with Annabelle at his side; she cast me a frightened glance. I didn't see the vampire anywhere, but that meant nothing.

Did the cabin seem older? Did it seem to be leaning slightly, its walls listing and unsteady? Did the trees seem different here as well?

I saw Niles' handheld, its screen crushed, lying in the dust. I picked it up. The glass marble was underneath, barely glowing--

In the sun. We were no longer *between.* We'd been pushed back into the normal world--if anything could be called normal anymore. The Human Realm.

"Niles!" I snapped his name and he raised his head and blinked at me. "You need to take my car and bring Sennet here. We may need her." I tossed him my keys. They landed far short, but Sam Rose picked them up, a question on his lips.

"What...where are you going?" Niles managed to ask.

"I'm going after Russ," I said, and picked up the marble.

Niles managed to raise himself up on his elbows. "But you're not--"

"A wizard," I said, and there was a moment of disorienting double vision before the world settled down again and I found myself *between* again. "Yes. I know."

Facing the cabin, not the icehouse. I started to turn around. Something pricked my back. As far as I knew, it could have been a sword.

"Who are you and why are you here?" a voice asked; a cracked and broken voice made thin by pain.

I raised my hands. "My name is Karen Montgomery," I said, keeping my voice soft and even. "I believe this is yours?" I turned, slowly, and held out the marble, which glowed brighter now, *between;* bright enough for me to see Joseph's white face; his hair was just as pale, his eyes colorless. His clothes hung in tatters. Almost, but not quite, a ghost.

"You were here before," he whispered, and held his hand out for the marble. I dropped it in his hand; he lowered his weapon, a long length of metal. Not a sword, but it would have hurt me badly nonetheless. "With *him.*" He nodded behind him, over his shoulder.

At the icehouse, which still remained rubble, even here.

I started past him. "Russ!"

Joseph caught my arm. Gasped a little, and almost fell forward, as if challenging me had used up all his strength. "He's...not there." He caught himself with the metal pole; I saw his other hand clench around the marble. "I got him out."

"You...you got him out?" I realized he was fading, and fast; his skin was almost translucent. "Is he--"

He tried to take a step. Automatically, I took his arm. He was so cold.

"He's not dead," he whispered, and fell into a boneless heap, his eyes closing, the faint reminders of roots still carved into his skin.

And I saw Russ behind him, laying in the grass, covered in dust, his skin gray, his eyes closed.

I left Joseph where he'd fallen and fell to my knees beside Russ. There were no obvious signs of trauma, save for a small streak of blood running down one side of his face. And he seemed to be breathing, but I dared not move him for fear of internal injuries. Or what if he'd broken his neck?

"Russ, can you hear me?" My voice cracked. A teardrop fell on his face and I reached out to wipe it away.

He caught my hand. Opened his eyes. Coughed. "Karen?"

I was still holding the handheld computer; I curled his hand around it. "I had to come back for you," I said, and tried not to let my voice shake.

"Someone...someone pulled me out," Russ whispered.

"Joseph did," I said. "He's--" I glanced back at him; he was glowing, faintly, in the darkness. "I think he's still alive."

"You...*think*?" Russ managed to roll over and sit up, leaning against me for support. He saw Joseph lying there and frowned. "Did he speak to you?"

"Yes, and he sounded quite coherent," I said. "We're back *between*, by the way; I sent Niles to find Sennet."

"Can he leave?" Russ asked.

I shrugged. "Does it matter? Healers go where they are needed."

Russ stared at me, a little shocked, I thought, but then he nodded. "True."

With my help, he managed to make it over to where Joseph lay, and knelt next to him. "He pulled me out."

"That's what he said." I touched Joseph's hand. "He's so cold."

Russ stared down at him for a moment, then pulled a penknife out of his pocket.

"What are you doing?" I asked, but then I knew. "Your blood heals vampires. But you said--"

"Is he still truly a vampire?" Russ asked. "I'm not sure. But it won't hurt to see if it helps. If he hasn't lost himself yet, then there's no reason not to save him." He sliced across his wrist; enough to bleed, but not enough to do any lasting harm. "And anyway, if Sennet *can't* come here, we might need his help to get back. You said you sent Niles--how?"

"We got knocked back into the human realm," I said. "When the tree blew up, or whatever happened."

Russ bent over to lift Joseph up and winced. "He *is* cold," he said, and pressed his bleeding wrist over Joseph's mouth.

For a moment, all I saw was blood, leaking down one side of Joseph's face, and then, almost imperceptibly, his throat moved. Swallowing. His hand moved; he curled it around Russ' wrist and frantically drank for a long few moments before he was aware enough to realize that Russ wasn't going to pull away.

And in fact, *he* pulled away before Russ was ready, gasping a little, his eyes clearer, but still colorless and pale. The blood on his lips was almost garish against the paleness of his skin.

Russ wrapped his wrist in a strip of cloth torn from his tattered shirt and I helped him knot the fabric. "I could give you more," he said. "Freely given, although I owe you my life."

"As I owe you mine," Joseph whispered. "Twice now." He coughed, his throat working, then reached up to wipe the blood away from his mouth.

"Do you remember what happened?" I asked.

Joseph frowned. "There was a wizard. A dead wizard." His eyes widened. "Josephine!"

He tried to rise, but Russ gently held him back. "Wait a minute," he said. "You...there's a lot you don't know. As far as *we* know, Josephine escaped."

"What year did you come here?" I asked gently.

Joseph stared at me. "I...you're going to tell me that it's been longer than I think, aren't you?"

"Your license expired fifty-two years ago," I said.

"I don't...I don't know what year my license expired," Joseph whispered. He rubbed his eyes; stared down at his hand. His other hand still clutched the marble.

"1958," I said.

It took him a moment to add up the years; to realize just how long he'd been trapped. His mouth opened in a soundless 'o' of shock. He drew his knees up against his chest and buried his face against them. His shoulders shook. The marble slipped from his fingers, no longer glowing, as if he'd sucked out all the magic; all the life from the glass. And as I watched, it crumbled and cracked into dust at his feet. And he did not seem to notice.

"I'm sorry," I said.

"It is not your fault," Joseph whispered. He raised his head, flexed his fingers. "Why is my skin so pale?"

"What do you remember about the tree?" Russ asked, and Joseph stared at him, and opened his mouth to reply--then, wondering, he traced the lines on his face; on his hands, on his arms. From the roots. And he bowed his head and wept.

The transition from *between* to the human realm seemed subtle, now; subtle save for the late afternoon sunlight that sparkled through the trees. I wasn't ready for that, but Russ erected another ward; the sunlight faded after a few minutes, though, and Joseph raised his head again.

And Sennet was there, with Niles and a blanket, which she draped over Joseph's shoulders and he clutched it around him, suddenly wary.

"I'm a Healer," she said, and he seemed to accept that; he didn't struggle when she helped him up, and he didn't pull away when her talent seeped under his skin.

"I don't have anywhere to go," he said when I helped him stand. He leaned on Sennet, still swaddled in the blanket, still unsteady on his feet.

"That's okay," Sennet said. "You can stay with me for as long as you need to." She glanced at us. "Russ?"

"I'm fine," Russ said.

"Come by my house later, okay? I'll fix your--" Sennet frowned at him. "Your leg?"

"Ankle, I think," Russ said, slightly breathless as he limped across the destruction to where Niles waited. "Maybe my knee, too."

"You could lean on me," I said, but he waved me away.

"I'll be fine." He kissed me to take the sting away from his words. "Really."

I saw Sam Rose and Annabelle standing in the shadows, watching as Sennet helped Joseph to her car. I left Russ leaning against the cabin wall with Niles at his side and walked to where they waited.

"*He* was responsible for this?" Annabelle asked.

"No," I said. "Not really. Not in the way you mean. I don't know the whole story yet, but he got caught in someone else's trap."

"And who was that someone else?" Sam Rose asked.

"Another wizard," I said. "One that built his cabin out of oak trees." I looked at Annabelle as I said this, and saw her blanch.

"There's one of your cousins--your kin--inside the cabin now," I said. "Do you think you could try to convince her to let Russ dig her up? With magic to ensure no root is broken?"

"Your *kin*?" Sam asked.

"How did you know?" Annabelle asked.

"Your tree was dead, *between*," I said. "And you said it was your monument."

"She won't listen to me, but I will speak to her," Annabelle said. "I should have joined those who have gone before when my tree died, but I did not. I was cut off from them. From their connection. Do you understand what that means?"

"I understand that is why you didn't want to be alone," I said. "And why you drove us away, before."

"If I am not with those who have gone before, then I will fade into nothingness," Annabelle whispered. "I *am* nothing."

"Would they take you back?" I asked.

Annabelle shook her head.

"Do *I* have to go?" Sam Rose asked.

I stared at him, momentarily confused. "What?"

"If Annabelle can't leave, then can I stay here with her?"

Annabelle gasped. "But I wasn't nice to you!"

"That doesn't mean you should have to spend the rest of eternity alone," Sam said resolutely.

"I don't have any say in that," I said. "I think it's your decision. No one here will force you to leave if you don't want to."

Sam nodded, but I don't think he really believed me.

"But I'm not sure what will happen to this place once we leave," I said. "Are you sure you want to stay?"

"I'm sure," Sam said, and took Annabelle's hand.

She clutched it, as if afraid he would vanish in front of her eyes. "I *have* to stay."

"Will you talk to your cousin?" I asked.

Annabelle smiled. "She is my sister," she said. "Long-lost, but still my sister. And yes. I will talk to her." She moved away from Sam, towards the cabin, said something to Russ when he asked her a question, and vanished inside.

"What now?" Sam Rose asked.

"There is no *between* anymore," I said, "At least not here. Perhaps the Council can keep your road invisible...that might be for the best, just in case you're both tied to your monuments."

"Yes, that might be for the best," Sam said. And then, awkwardly, "Thank you."

I smiled. "You're welcome."

I noticed Ethan, then, standing in the middle of the driveway with a brown paper bag in one hand and a slightly amused look on his face. He held up the bag when he caught my eye.

"Healers can be pushy."

"Yes, they can," I said, and waited until he made his way to where I stood. "What did she tell you?"

"That I needed to bring Russ something to drink because otherwise he'll collapse and she'll have to get a bigger house," he said. "And to not to let him do anything stupid. Does she realize how hard that might be?"

"If stupid means trying to save a life, then he'll never agree with that," I said. "Ethan, this is Sam."

"You're--" Ethan began.

"A ghost," Sam Rose said. "Essentially." He held out his hand; Ethan hesitated, then shook it. Then looked surprised and shocked, all at the same time.

Russ had noticed Ethan's presence; he stayed where he was, and I realized he was hurting now; that last burst of adrenalin had worn off. But he managed to smile as we approached.

"Maybe I *will* lean on you," he whispered.

"Anytime," I said, and took his arm. He sagged against me.

"Sennet ordered me to bring you something to drink," Ethan said, and I heard the ghost of old guilt in his voice.

I helped Russ sit down. Niles sat beside us; Ethan handed Russ the bottle and the cup and we waited while he drank. And then he fell asleep, nestled at my side.

"He should be resting," Ethan said quietly. "He needs to--"

"We're waiting on Annabelle," I told him. "There are a few loose ends."

"What *happened?*" Ethan asked, and we told him; Sam Rose and Niles and I, while Russ slept.

After a while, Annabelle emerged from the cabin. She stood behind us until Sam noticed her; he motioned her into our group.

"She will--" Annabelle looked as if she'd been crying. "She will make the attempt."

"Niles, could you do it if Russ isn't--" I said, but Russ replied before I could finish my sentence.

"I'm fine," he said. "You might have to carry me out of here afterwards, but I have enough strength for the attempt." He raised his head and stared at us, almost challenging someone to say otherwise.

I glanced at Ethan. He met my gaze and nodded.

"I'm going to need a really big pot," Russ said, and I helped him to his feet.

"I think Niles and I can handle that part of the preparations," Ethan said.

"We...what?" Niles asked. He looked tired, too, which was only to be expected.

"Come with me," Ethan said, and held out his hand to help Niles up. "We'll be back shortly."

Annabelle and Sam moved off together to wait. I helped Russ into the cabin. The dryad stood beside her tree, her hands clasped together, as if in prayer.

"I'll have to touch your tree," Russ said, his voice soft. "I promise I'll be gentle."

She nodded. "My kin told me I should grow strong. That it's not a bad thing to be uprooted. That I could find better soil somewhere else."

"That's true," I said.

"She also said she chose her own name. But she took that name from the human ghost's memories, and I do not want to do the same."

From Russ', I realized.

"I don't think my daughter would mind if you shared her name," Russ said, and settled down beside the tree. "Her name was Rosemarie."

"I know," the dryad whispered. "I saw."

Russ closed his eyes and leaned against the wall. He touched the tree's tiny trunk, and I saw a spark of something leave his hand and travel across the wood and down the trunk until it vanished into the ground.

The dryad shivered. "That tickles!"

The handheld was broken; its screen cracked. Russ used it anyway, projecting a picture in the air instead of on the screen, showing the delicate network of roots below.

There really weren't that many. Nothing like the ones that had imprisoned Joseph.

But it took time to shelter all of them, nonetheless. Ethan returned without Niles almost an hour later, bearing a large plastic pot.

"I hope this is big enough," he said to me.

"I think it will be," I said. "Where's Niles?"

"I left him with Aden, resting." He set the pot on the ground. "Russ?"

"There," Russ breathed, and opened his eyes.

The tree was glowing now; softly illuminating the shadows around us. Russ made a motion with one hand and the tree neatly emerged from the ground--with soil still around its roots--every threadlike piece encased in his spell.

The dryad gasped as Russ lowered her tree and its rootball into the pot.

"We'll find a nice place for you to live and flourish," I promised.

"There's a meadow near your house," Russ murmured.

"It's not my house," I said.

"It *will* be," Russ replied, and I didn't deny his words, because I hoped they were true.

"Let me help you up," I said, and extended my hand.

He leaned against me when he stood, barely putting any weight on his left leg. "Ethan, could you carry the tree?"

"Of course," Ethan said. "Do you want me to drive? I took Karen's car--"

"Yes," I said. "Please."

We piled in together, the dryad and her tree in the front seat beside Ethan, Russ in the back with me. Annabelle and Sam watched us go from the end of the driveway; both waved.

They seemed happy. I wished them well.

Later, after Sennet saw to Russ and sent him home to rest, after Niles bunked on the couch and Aden slept in the only spare bedroom in Russ' house, Ethan and I carried the tiny oak tree into the meadow beside the stone house, dug a hole, and gently introduced Rosemarie to her new home.

Even in the darkness, the stone house seemed welcoming. I lingered, staring, until Ethan laughed.

"I thought he was awake when we left," he said, and I saw someone sitting on the porch now, a shadow in the darkness.

He rose as we approached. "I would have preferred to be there to help," Russ said, but there was no heat in his words; no blame.

"We managed," Ethan told him. "Are you..."

"I'm fine," Russ said. "A little sore, but that will pass." He glanced at me. "Sennet called. Joseph will be awake by dusk tomorrow; she said if we wanted to talk to him, we could come then."

"That sounds good," I said, and saw two bags beside him; and a coffee pot. "Are we staying here tonight?"

"I thought that would be best," Russ said. "Ethan needs a place to sleep--"

Ethan opened his mouth, perhaps to protest that he could very well use the floor, but then he shut it again and nodded at the house. "Karen told me a bit about the rules," he said. "Are you sure you want to risk--"

Russ took my hand. "If we're going to be together, Peter will have to get used to me," he said.

"I agree," I said.

"Well, then. I'll see if Niles will bring you breakfast," Ethan said, and we watched him walk down the overgrown driveway.

"Is there electricity for that coffeemaker?" I asked.

"There's magic," Russ said.

I smiled. "That will do."

The End

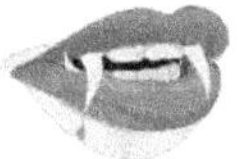

You can find ALL our books up on our website at:

http://www.writers-exchange.com

All Jennifer's books:

http://www.writers-exchange.com/Jennifer-St-Clair/

all our fantasy novels:

http://www.writers-exchange.com/category/genres/fantasy/

About the Author

Jennifer St. Clair grew up in Southern Ohio and spent most of her childhood in the woods around her home. She wrote her first novel when she was thirteen, and hasn't stopped since. She lives with her ball python, Fester, and two cats, Ash and Rowan.

In her spare time, she crochets, makes cloth dolls, collects antiques, books, and vintage clothing, and takes digital photographs with varying degrees of success.

Her *Beth-Hill series* is set in the area in America that contains many supernatural creatures: Wild Hunt, Vampires, Dragons, Faery and more.

It is part of the Universe that her *Jacob Lane Series, Karen Montgomery Series* and vampire trilogy, *The Shadow Series* are set in.

Follow all her books on her author page:

http://www.writers-exchange.com/Jennifer-St-Clair/

If you want to read more about other books by this author, they are listed on the following pages...

A Beth-Hill Novel (Stand Alone Novels)

Are creatures of the night and all manner of extramundane beings drawn to certain locations in the natural world? In the Midwestern village of Beth-Hill located in southern Ohio, the population is made up of its fair share of common citizens...and much more than its share of supernatural residents. Take a walk on the wild side in this unusual place where imagination meets reality.

Blood of Innocents

Ten years ago, Orien, crown prince of the Seleighe, was captured by his mortal enemies, locked in a dungeon and turned into a vampire. Six years into Orien's sentence, the Healer's brother Cullen disobeyed his mistress's orders to kill him and turned him into a vampire instead, thus sealing both their fates for all eternity.

Now both Orien and Cullen are set free. But a secret only Cullen knows lies locked inside his mind, threatening to drive him mad before he can uncover the identity of a traitor--the very elf who betrayed Orien and left them both to die in darkness.

Publisher: http://www.writers-exchange.com/blood-of-innocents/

Full Moon

Werewolves change into wolves when the moon is full. But Edward's curse only allows him to be *human* when the moon is full.

Alone and despairing, Edward hides himself away from the world. He's scraped out a meager existence for himself for almost a century in the forest he's grown to love and call home. But in the depths of a terrible winter, he stumbles across clues from the life his mother left behind in Faerie. The truth may give him the answers he needs about the source of his birthright... and the curse that holds him captive.

Publisher: http://www.writers-exchange.com/full-moon/

A Beth-Hill Novel: Jacob Lane Series

Are creatures of the night and all manner of extramundane beings drawn to certain locations in the natural world? In the Midwestern village of Beth-Hill located in southern Ohio, the population is made up of its fair share of common citizens...and much more than its share of supernatural residents.

Jacob Lane is a ten-year-old girl who's spent her life unaware of her magical heritage. After being sent to Darkbrook, a school of magic, supernatural mysteries seem to spring to life all around her and her new friends.

Book 1: The Tenth Ghost

After Jacob Lane's parents mysteriously vanish, she's sent to Darkbrook, the only school of magic in the United States. While there, she and her new friends stumble upon a series of mysterious deaths in the nine ghosts that haunt the halls of Darkbrook. These ghosts were students who died at the school over the past hundred years. Will Jacob become the tenth ghost, or can she stop a witch's reign of terror?

Publisher: http://www.writers-exchange.com/the-tenth-ghost/

Book 2: The Ninth Guest

When Jacob's friend Ophelia's family decides to open up their castle for guests, amateur paranormal sleuth Jacob Lane is invited to join in on the fun. "Spend the night in a vampire's castle and live to tell the tale!" is supposed to be a fundraiser to help Ophelia's family pay the bills. Heating a castle costs quite a bit, after all. But, after the truth of an old secret is uncovered, what began as an innocent business venture soon turns deadly when vampire hunters get involved.

For years, the vampire hunters have had only one goal: To destroy all vampires. With the help of a new friend, Jacob and Ophelia must work together to save the entire VonBriggle family from extinction.

Publisher: http://www.writers-exchange.com/the-ninth-guest/

Book 3: The Eighth Room

For two hundred years, the Selkies have kept themselves separate from those who live on land. But now the Selkies need allies or they'll be crushed by their ancient enemies, the Finfolk.

Jacob and Ophelia, students at the only school of magic in the United States, uncover a mystery that dates back to Darkbrook's beginnings. While helping clean out old storage rooms for classroom expansion, they find something that might save the Selkies from extinction. With the help of the youngest member of the Wild Hunt who are no longer so wild or terrifying, they must foil the Finfolk who desire the Selkie's destruction...or die trying.

Publisher: http://www.writers-exchange.com/the-eighth-room/

Book 4: The Seventh Secret

After a picture of Niklas, the dragons' liaison to the only school of magic in the United States, shows up in too many newspapers to count, Darkbrook is forced to go on the defensive. The secret of Darkbrook's existence has been discovered. But there are more than dragonhunters in the forest, and, as Jacob Lane, supernatural sleuth and student at Darkbrook, learns how to use her newly discovered talent of healing, she helps to right an old wrong and must battle a teenaged wizard intent on proving--once and for all--that magic is real.

Publisher: http://www.writers-exchange.com/the-seventh-secret/

Book 5: The Sixth Stone

Jacob Lane, supernatural sleuth, and Danny, her werewolf friend, stumble across an alternate world where the Wild Hunt was never bound, and Darkbrook, the school of magic they attend, was abandoned a hundred years ago.

But when the Hounds of the Hunt wish to surrender, the two students are swept up in a whirlwind of heartbreak, betrayal, and the discovery of a lost treasure.

Publisher: http://www.writers-exchange.com/the-sixth-stone/

A Beth-Hill Novella: Karen Montgomery Series

Are creatures of the night and all manner of extramundane beings drawn to certain locations in the natural world? In the Midwestern village of Beth-Hill located in southern Ohio, the population is made up of its fair share of common citizens...and much more than its share of supernatural residents. Take a walk on the wild side in this unusual place where imagination meets reality.

Karen Montgomery was an ordinary woman until she stumbled into the extraordinary... A bargain with elves worth its weight in gold. A plague of sinister ladybugs. Rogue vampire hunters, including one who tries to turn over a new leaf--with disastrous consequences. A ghostly huntsmen of the Wild Hunt wishing for redemption. Karen's life will never be the same again.

Book 1: Budget Cuts

Karen Montgomery is used to taking care of the unpleasant jobs no one else wants to deal with. When a shortage of funds forces her to fire fifteen employees from the library, she isn't happy, but the nasty task has to be done and she is, after all, the boss. But Karen finds finishing her task impossible when she can't seem to track down Ivy Bedinghaus, a night clerk she's never actually met. Once she finally does confront Ivy, she's thrust into a centuries-old conflict that makes her previous troubles radically pale in comparison.

Publisher: http://www.writers-exchange.com/budget-cuts/

Book 2: The Secret of Redemption

Karen Montgomery, librarian, finds herself embroiled in another otherworldly adventure...

A member of the Wild Hunt--ghostly myths that aren't so ghostly (or myth-like) anymore--needs help in reconciling who he once was in life and who he is now.

A little girl has gone missing. And the one most likely responsible for her disappearance is the one Karen must prove innocent.

Publisher: http://www.writers-exchange.com/the-secret-of-redemption/

Book 3: Ladybug, Ladybug

An innocent attempt to rid the library of a plague of ladybugs turns sinister when a rogue vampire hunter gets the contract for pest control.

Ivy Bedinghaus, who works for Karen as a night clerk--along with all the vampires in Beth-Hill--are in danger, and their only hope for survival is with the help of Karen, a member of the Wild Hunt, and Russell Moore, a reformed vampire hunter.

Publisher: http://www.writers-exchange.com/ladybug-ladybug/

Book 4: Detour

One wrong turn sends Karen down a road that shouldn't exist, to the site of an old accident and an even older mystery. With reformed vampire hunter Russell Moore's help, Karen finds the key to the mystery. But Russ keeps his own secrets...some of which are deadly.

When old friends from Russ' past come to call, Karen realizes his secrets might just mean his doom. After a terrible incident three years ago, before Karen met him, Russ wants only to live the rest of his life quietly in Beth-Hill. But his secret might not allow him the new lease on life Russ longs for.

Publisher: http://www.writers-exchange.com/detour/

Companion Story: Russ' Story: Capture

Long before Russell Moore ever met supernatural sleuth Karen Montgomery or set foot in Beth-Hill, he was a vampire hunter, possibly the best vampire hunter of all. He brought down whole nests of vampires, caring little about the consequences of his actions. Anyone who lived with or helped the vampires became enemies to be slaughtered.

So what kind of an idiot would capture a ruthless vampire hunter without a conscience and try to reform him?

Ethan Walker was that idiot. Wanting to protect his family, Ethan set out to prove to Russ that vampires weren't all evil, soulless creatures. If Russ would allow himself to witness their lives, see their humanity, surely he and other vampire hunters like him would let them live in peace. *Surely?*

Publisher: http://www.writers-exchange.com/capture/

Secrets When in Shadow Lie

Twelve years ago, Ryan Grey was cursed by a witch to hide a secret. He's lived with the curse of being unable to die permanently, and, over the years he's slowly losing the memory of his past until almost nothing remains.

But now, after a chance meeting with an elf named Zipporah, he discovers the key to unlocking the secret and breaking the curse once and for all...if he can survive the breaking.

Publisher: http://www.writers-exchange.com/secrets-when-in-shadow-lie/

The Dead Who Do Not Sleep

Will Spark only wants a good night's sleep after a night of drinking. Instead, two thugs bang on his door, demanding answers to questions he can't understand. And then they killed him...

Publisher: http://www.writers-exchange.com/the-dead-who-do-not-sleep/

A Beth-Hill Novel: The Abby Duncan Series

Are creatures of the night and all manner of extramundane beings drawn to certain locations in the natural world? In the Midwestern village of Beth-Hill located in southern Ohio, the population is made up of its fair share of common citizens...and much more than its share of supernatural residents. Take a walk on the wild side in this unusual place where imagination meets reality.

Situated in Beth-Hill, where imagination meets reality, is The Rose Emporium, owned by elderly and not-a-little-odd Rose Duncan. The large Victorian house smackdab in the middle of nowhere is a cross between a pawn shop and an antique store that caters to supernatural creatures needing to barter. Rose's twenty-something niece, Abby Duncan, discovers that the world isn't made up of just run-of-the-mill, ordinary humans but an entire spectrum of unusual beings. With her preconceptions about what's normal and what's not turned upside-down, Abby is in for a whole lot of startling truths, mysteries-- about herself and the people and places around her--and danger.

Novella 1: By Any Other Name

Woodturner Abby Duncan decides to sell her spindles at a local Renaissance Festival with only some success. After all, no one really spins their own yarn anymore, do they? While there, she discovers that one of her newfound friends is not what he appears--and his secret is about to get him killed!

Publisher: http://www.writers-exchange.com/by-any-other-name/

Book 2: The Uncrowned Queen

Abby Duncan's elderly Aunt Rose has always been a bit odd. And now she's off on a mysterious trip, leaving Abby behind to run the Rose Emporium, an unusual sort of antique shop. Such an extraordinary store would have been a perfect place for Seth and the others, her friends from the Renaissance Festival, to take a break from traveling between Faires. But when tragedy strikes and Abby and the others discover the true nature of the Rose Emporium, they'll have to travel into Faerie itself before their tightknit group is whole again.

Abby doesn't know much about her family history, but she's about to find out the truth...whether she likes it or not.

Publisher: http://www.writers-exchange.com/the-uncrowned-queen/

Book 3: Coming Soon!

A Beth-Hill Novel: The Shadows Trilogy

Are creatures of the night and all manner of extramundane beings drawn to certain locations in the natural world? In the Midwestern village of Beth-Hill located in southern Ohio, the population is made up of its fair share of common citizens...and much more than its share of supernatural residents. Take a walk on the wild side in this unusual place where imagination meets reality.

A Dreamer dreams the future when the past is not yet laid to rest. Ten years ago, a plague swept across the Seven Kingdoms. Ten years ago, the Queen of Iomar's son was exiled and named the author of the magical plague. Now, in the present, Terrin works to complete his ultimate goal: Control of the Seven Kingdoms using his son's power to supplement his own. But his attempt at dominion meets resistance and the fate of the world rests in the unlikely hands of an exiled prince, a Dreamer, and a vampire...

Book 1: The Prince of Shadows

When Alban's father Terrin appeared at the castle door with a vampire in tow and apologies on his lips, Alban fell under his spell just like everyone else and welcomed him home. But Terrin didn't return to live quietly in his brother's kingdom. He had other plans and, with Alban's untrained powers at his disposal, he begins his ruthless plan to destroy the Seven Kingdoms and rule them all, beginning with his brother's death.

Terrin engineers events to cast the blame on his nephew, Teluride, intending to see the boy executed for his father's murder. But there are those who would thwart Terrin in his mad plan for power, and Alban forms an unlikely alliance with Skade, the reclusive Queen of Iomar, and Terrin's slave, a young vampire with no memory of his name or origins. Although the future looks grim, Alban and the vampire attempt to stop Terrin...and they almost succeed.

A darker history lies at the heart of Terrin's treachery, and only Skade knows the true reason why Terrin would murder his own brother and attempt to destroy both Alban and the vampire to achieve his goals. The Ghost who resides in Skade's mirror--her servant and thrall--holds one of the keys to Terrin's madness. Unfortunately, more than one person wishes for the past to remain the past and the future to hold no shadows of what might have been...

Publisher: http://www.writers-exchange.com/the-prince-of-shadows/

Book 2: Lost In Shadows

Events set in motion ten years ago come to a head as Skade, the reclusive Queen of Iomar, and Nicodemus, who is imprisoned by Skade, struggle to free Alban and the vampire from Terrin's grasp. Old secrets come to light when Skade's exiled son is forced to face his past--or die trying to redeem himself once and for all. Can the crimes of the past truly be forgiven? Only time will tell...and time is running out.

Publisher: http://www.writers-exchange.com/lost-in-shadows/

Book 3: Bound In Shadows

With his power crushed, brother to the king and father to Alban, Terrin is forced to take drastic measures to regain his sons after they are freed and harness the power they possess. But he has an ally inside the healer's house where they are recovering who works to further his plans. The Queen of Iomar, Skade's son, courts redemption to try to save his mother's life, and the vampire who no longer remembers his own name dreams a dream that might save them all...or damn them if success is thwarted.

Publisher: http://www.writers-exchange.com/bound-in-shadows/

A Beth-Hill Novel: Wild Hunt Series

Are creatures of the night and all manner of extramundane beings drawn to certain locations in the natural world? In the Midwestern village of Beth-Hill located in southern Ohio, the population is made up of its fair share of common citizens...and much more than its share of supernatural residents. Take a walk on the wild side in this unusual place where imagination meets reality.

The Wild Hunt roamed the forest outside of Beth-Hill until the Council bound them for a hundred years. Nevertheless, a century of existence has made an indelible mark not easily forgotten for these ghostly myths that are no longer so ghostly or myth-like...

Book 1: Heart's Desire

The Wild Hunt roamed the forest outside of Beth-Hill until the Council bound them for a hundred years--a lifetime for a human but only a passing thought to one such as Gabriel, Master of the Wild Hunt. As the Council's binding draws to a close, old enemies reappear to ensure that the Wild Hunt is bound once more--to a creature much worse than the Council has been.

Publisher: http://www.writers-exchange.com/hearts-desire/

Book 2: Fire and Water

As a young vampire, Erialas Morgan brought his mother back to life with a spell that shouldn't exist, shouldn't have worked...perhaps shouldn't have been performed at all. Desperation and love are his only excuses for doing the unthinkable.

There are others who wish to use that same spell for their own gain--and to destroy the Wild Hunt once and for all. Caught in the middle of a war between the Morgan clan of vampires and their human kin, Erialas turns to the Hunt for help. But even Gabriel, the Master of the Wild Hunt, may not be able to stop the tide of death and destruction once it turns.

Publisher: http://www.writers-exchange.com/fire-and-water/

Book 3: The Lost

Almost sixty years ago, Darkbrook, the only school of magic in the United States, opened its doors to students of decidedly different natures, sending out letters of invitation to the elves, the dragons, and the vampires. The three who responded to the invitation banded together despite their differences but vanished only weeks later along with an entire classroom full of students and their teacher after a field trip gone horribly wrong.

The Wild Hunt has healed and the Hounds have grown closer together, keeping Darkbrook's forest safe and secure for those who live there. Malachi, one of the eldest members of the Wild Hunt, has adapted to Josiah's spell to help him see, but when a demon boy trapped in the body of a human body for sixty years inside the school disrupts the newfound calm, the Hunt--and those they protect--are thrust into a struggle that should have ended long ago when a vampire, an elf, and a dragon vanished into the Mists.

Publisher: http://www.writers-exchange.com/the-lost/

Book 4: A Glint of Silver

Jericho is a vampire who wants is to live away from the Richmond household of vampires led by his ruthless father Connor. When Jericho tries to escape, Connor punishes him and leaves him to die. Tristan is determined to be the one to bring Jericho back, but he can't see him suffer for wanting a normal life. As long as Connor lives, Jericho will never be safe or free. As long as Connor *lives...*

Publisher: http://www.writers-exchange.com/a-glint-of-silver/

Book 5: All That Glitters

As a member of the cruel Morgan Household of vampires, twelve-year-old Arthur Morgan has been abused all his life.

Maya, a water fairy, shows him just how horrible and twisted the household he's grown up is. With her help, and the unexpected help of an adult vampire, Arthur attempts to escape.

Can he become something more than what his father has decreed?

Publisher: http://www.writers-exchange.com/all-that-glitters/

The Chelsea Chronicles

Normally a quiet, serene place, Chelsea Kingdom seems like the perfect location for a centuries' old vampire to blend in and live a normal life, even escape hunters and an angry mob. Unfortunately, his timing couldn't be worse...

Book 1: So You Want to be a Vampire

Chelsea Kingdom is usually a pretty quiet place but recent murders--committed by a vampire--upset the calm. Newcomer to town, Vlad Dhalgren wants only to blend in and live a normal life. He quickly learns that isn't possible, given that other vampires have been hiding in the shadows around the castle--in plain sight--for years.

Despite her lineage, Anna Everett, the crown princess of the Kingdom of Chelsea, isn't a wizard like her father, which means she will never be Queen. She has only one friend, Valerian Moreton--Val--who has secrets he's never shared that could get him *and* Anna killed...

Publisher: http://www.writers-exchange.com/so-you-want-to-be-a-vampire/

Book 2: Transformation

As Anna, crown princess of Chelsea, adjusts to life as a vampire after recent events, Vlad plans for a future he has no real hope to seeing come to pass due to injuries sustained while attempting to save Anna's life. But, as life goes on for Anna and her friend Valerian "Val" Moreton, it changes for others--some of whom are not quite what they seem...

Publisher: http://www.writers-exchange.com/transformation/

You can find ALL our books up on our website at:

http://www.writers-exchange.com

All Jennifer's books:

http://www.writers-exchange.com/Jennifer-St-Clair/

all our fantasy novels:

http://www.writers-exchange.com/category/genres/fantasy/